I0733904

Cindy M. Amos

LIFTING LOCK RUNNER

By Cindy M. Amos

Landscapes of Mercy, Book 5

Let your thanksgiving flow along an endless canal
for the love He extends to
the brotherhood of boaters;
His love is aimed for you and
His deeds promise to be more generous
than the lake's depths.
Psalm 107:31

Cindy M. Amos

ISBN-13:978-1-946939-04-3

Dedicated to
Parker M. Amos & Cameron H. Amos
My Florida-born sons who treasured our trips
to the locks of Lake Okeechobee
Once upon a childhood ago in the land
of perpetual sunshine

The author would like to acknowledge the following
for their support and encouragement with this book:
iStock.com for Port Mayaca cover photograph
Pamela Bower, Proofreader
Janice Fairbairn, Marketing Strategist for LOM
Series
Cynthia Hickey of Forget Me Not Romances
& Inspiration of the Holy Spirit

LANDSCAPES OF MERCY SERIES BOOK FIVE

Yet there is one ray of hope:
God's compassion never ends.
Only the Lord's mercies have kept us
from complete destruction.
Great is His faithfulness;
His lovingkindness renews each day.
Lamentations 3:21-23

Chapter 1

Her gaze scanning the lock chamber, Fallon McKenzie signaled the tower and the water began to flow in torrents. St. Lucie Locks had drawn a fair crowd this morning as May dwindled toward the holiday weekend. Two boats sat in the chamber below heading west for Lake Okeechobee in the heart of Florida, as a stream of pedestrian day visitors came across the concrete walkway atop the chamber gate. She smiled despite the repetitive routine and followed procedure to visually inspect the vessels.

Two small boats gamboled about the outer wall of the lock due to the flooding of the chamber. With the water level of Lake Okeechobee standing at 14 feet, the chamber would require all twenty minutes of their estimated time-in-lock to bring the waters of the St. Lucie River up to canal level. The occupants of the boats traded shouts as the waters roared from the gates up ahead. A teenage girl in the rear boat seemed to be receiving coaching on how to tighten her stern line against the cleat as the vessel floated up. The front boat's male occupant moved fluidly from bow to stern, making his line adjustments like second nature.

Temporarily distracted by a young mother with two preschoolers on the breezeway, Fallon found chaos had paid an unwelcome visit down below. The gray-haired man with the teenager now slumped over the helm. Several shouts followed and, before she could surmise the proper course of action, the first boater unfastened his bow line and allowed his boat to swing backward to bridge the gap between vessels.

Grabbing for her radio, she walked down the chamber's flank to gain a better perspective. "Loose boat, Charlie. Better slow the gates." She hated to draw out the process, but havoc was no respecter of time. Her world shrank to a rectangle of churning water where two small boats floundered in the swirl of incoming waters. The pitch of the roar stepped back a notch and the turbulence lessened about the time the rescuer abandoned ship for the craft in peril. "Stand by for a possible medical issue."

Down below, the younger man pulled the gray-haired captain off the helm and placed him in the floor of the boat. Recognizing the early phase of CPR, she gave the radio code for medical emergency, which triggered the procedure for calling nine-one-one. The teen had coiled up in a fetal ball on the back bench, missing her interval of shortening the stern line to hold the boat taut against the lock wall.

Fallon motioned with her arms and shouted a command to tighten the line through cupped hands. By some miracle, the girl responded and pulled with both arms to shorten the poly rope. She motioned the girl forward and watched her struggle past the two men to comply. A tap on her knee proved to be Charlie. He dropped a megaphone and ran back toward the tower.

"Put the girl in the forward boat," Fallon said with paced pronunciation through the amplified instrument. "If you can man both lines there, I'll have the gates opened wider so we can get you out sooner." The rescuer stood and signaled, then stepped to the bow to steady the teenager as she jumped into the vacant craft. Both went to work tightening lines.

Fallon pulled the radio and gave instructions to increase the flow. They had seven minutes of scramble to get the gate open on the canal side for the rescue to progress. The pedestrians wouldn't expect such a rapid closure of the walkway, so she jogged up the chamber flank to make an announcement.

"Ladies and gentlemen, may I have your attention please? Due to a medical emergency in the lock below, we're accelerating the water flow to get our rescue teams to the vessels in need. That will close the pedestrian access in seven minutes, but I see a sailboat coming up the river that represents our next cycle. Please enjoy the north shore of St. Lucie Locks in the interim and make your way off the gate platform at this time. Your full cooperation is appreciated."

Several children ran to the far side of the concrete pass, causing their parents to jog after them. Time stalled at ground level while it churned frantically down below. She hastened the pedestrian migration until everyone had exited the structure safely.

A water level gauge painted onto the concrete flank told her the filling process had run three-quarters of its depth. The rescuer worked with a rhythm, pulling the stern line into compliance, stopping to check his victim and apply heart massages, and then finishing with a bow line adjustment where he encouraged the teen.

A siren split the air making Fallon's heart skip a beat as she exited the manmade walkway for solid land. The gates opened prematurely and a crest of water shoved into the lock, equalizing the water level which caused the boats to buck like plastic toys."Get the girl back in and bring them to the dock port-side."

She leveraged her weight against the upper cleat to release the bow line. The rescuer waved and set to work retrieving the teen as the slack line cascaded around them. Charlie beat her to the stern connection and tossed the line into the boat as it drifted off the wall. The outboard motor stirred to take control.

She ran to direct the arriving medics, sprinting toward the canal dock. Landlocked visitors murmured from the north shore, but she focused on the victim as she tried to outrun time. An ambulance pulled in toward the campground followed by a lime green pick-up truck with county markings. She motioned toward the dock and disappeared down the ramp. *How long had it been—seven minutes or more?*

Her feet slipped on wet boards left from dock anglers earlier when the fishing had been decent. Locking her knees to steady her trunk, Fallon glanced into the boat. The teenager cried hysterically as they approached the dock, but managed to throw the bow line at her. It felt electrified.

She tethered the boat and stepped over the gunwale, reaching the downed boatman. Her fingertips dug for a pulse at the base of his neck, but the nudging of the boat against the dock confused the reading. Charlie arrived dockside and retrieved the girl.

The rattle of a gurney down the dock ramp echoed in her ears as the rescuer knelt beside her. His features struck her as disarming up close, with caramel brown hair under his cap and soft brown eyes anticipating her instruction. His gaze lingered a mesmerizing moment.

She nodded while fighting to stay focused. "Straddle the gunwale and hold us onto the dock so they can gain access." An ashen shade of gray-green, the old man had lacked circulation for some time. Now touch-and-go for him, the worst place anyone could have a heart attack would be in the canal lock. The gurney rattled and banked toward the boat when a husky man in uniform came aboard in front of the rescuer. She yielded position to the medic and fought her cramped knees to stand.

"No detectable pulse," she relayed. "It started about eight minutes ago inside the lock. We'd just started flooding when he collapsed over the helm. This gentleman on the gunwale stepped over from the other watercraft and began administering CPR right away."

"That might have saved him, as I've got a weak pulse," he replied, motioning for assistance.

Fallon stepped aft to clear the space. The original rescuer caught her elbow and moved her out of the boat, their faces passing inches apart. His grip iron strong, her magnetic compass pegged in his direction and she blushed, right there with one foot on the dock.

Charlie mistook her hesitation for a stumble and came to her, pulling her from the rescuer to get her on land.

A sob above the ramp fell as a cue to redirect her usefulness, so she hurried up to ground level to take the teen in her arms. Tears fell on her shoulder as the EMTs strapped the victim to the gurney and brought him up the ramp. "I need to ask you for your names for my report and then you can ride with the ambulance."

"He's my grandfather, Mel Atkins. I'm Heather and I do want to stay with him. But what will happen to our boat?" The medics halted at the back of the ambulance and folded the gurney inside.

"Here, take this and call me when you get settled," she replied, handing her the contact card. "I'm Fallon McKenzie with the Corps of Engineers. Trust me with the boat until then." She turned the girl's shoulders toward the lime green truck where the county personnel secured her inside. For the first time since the man collapsed, she stood idle, her senses heightened by the urgent chain of events. Sweat streamed down her back.

"Fallon?" a man's voice called behind her. Something liquid swept through her, leaving her knees unsteady. The rescuer approached her as Charlie hunkered back to the tower.

In her peripheral vision, a sailboat's mast poked the sky, demanding attention on the lower end as the water flowed down the St. Lucie Canal. The ambulance departed, lights flaring down the access road.

His face thawed with a hint of charm at the corners of his lips. "I'm Court Reynolds with Bait Crate Fishing Supplies. Let me tow the old man's boat to Lake Okeechobee. I can get Jake at the Fish Camp to hold it for me behind the store."

A low tone sounded from the tower as her gaze swept the canal to assess traffic on the high end. Nothing seemed pressing. "I'm afraid two boats and one man doesn't equate to a successful formula for making it through the next lock at Port Mayaca. Right now, we need to get your boat out of the lock chamber. Meet me here on the dock afterward and we'll discuss other options for getting Mr. Atkins' boat secured. I need to touch base with Charlie."

"Sure thing," he replied, turning in the same direction she'd stepped. His hand rubbed across her forearm as the slightest gesture of compliance. "Hope the old man's going to pull out of this. The summer's just starting…plenty of good fishing left to enjoy."

She contemplated the thin-edged difference between ending and starting, thinking to fling a short prayer heavenward for the man's recovery. "One thing I've learned from working here at the locks is that time is seldom on your side."

A seaman's whistle split the air and Charlie waved, having gaffed the front cleat on Court's bow and brought it around. The boat owner jogged toward the reunion. The aging lock tender gave the man a hearty slap on his shoulder for the rescue, and saluted as he shoved the vessel off the wall. The boat engine stirred and the craft soon made forward progress.

Every ounce of her wanted to pull out of the lock with him, leaving her station work behind. Forcing her feet back to the tower, she hadn't noticed Liam Ware striding over from the campground supervised by his mother on the south shore. Having an extra warm body might come in handy with the pending boat tow, and she looked at the shaggy-haired teen with scrutiny. Fate would not allow for an outright swap of duty. It became apparent she'd have to man the fort and send this green-behind-the-ears galley swab with Court Reynolds instead.

"Hey, Liam. Want to give us a hand by going on a

boat ride up to Lake O? We had a medical emergency and the guy's boat will be in the way down here."

His face made the trip from flat-out bored to all-out inspired in seconds. "I'll ask mom." He smiled, revealing two front teeth at odds with one another. "It'd sure break up my day."

"Tell Sheri it would help us out. I'm stuck here with Charlie until Emmitt arrives." The teen ran back across the access road, a reminder that she should get going, too. She opened the door and assaulted the steel steps to the lookout platform. Reaching the upper deck, she gauged the approach of the sailboat and then turned to check traffic up the canal. Two fishing boats lolled about in the canal, but no one pressed for service. They would keep the cycle open until the request came from the sailboat, standard operating procedure.

A sensation pulling at her heart didn't seem too standard, as the handsome rescuer waited for her by the dock. Liam could steer the boat in tow behind Court. They didn't need a third party, though she did have a canal survey to conduct between here and Port Mayaca. She checked the time on her cell phone and devised a plan that included her. Depending on how accommodating Court would be, she could tag along to make her mandatory journal entries and record water depths along the way. Feasible, it would save gas and wear on their equipment, if only she could leave Charlie shorthanded without any guilt.

As Court knelt on the dock securing his bow line, she noticed the large bait box on his stern for the first time. He traveled with a host of company already, most likely a vault full of silvery shiners to outfox the hungry bass in the lake. He would likely make the rounds along the shore, outfitting the bait stores and fish camps with live bait. That would make her tagalong all the more interesting, as the district needed to scout the lake levels as well. Convinced that it made too much sense not to go, she descended to reason with Charlie.

Liam jabbed his thumb westward. "I'm going to the lake."

Charlie nodded and motioned toward the dock. "You'd be good help, young man,"

Fallon cleared her throat, stepping into the huddle to launch into her justification speech.

"You ought to ride along too, Fallon," Charlie added. "We could knock out that monthly shoreline survey if you record the water levels. Wouldn't even have to operate the boat, just record the readings. Makes too much sense not to do it, so don't argue with me about it."

Her expression must have reflected her relinquishment of duty as he leaned closer.

"I'll call Emmitt and have him come in early. He needs the hours anyway. And you need to shake free of this place once in a while. Be a saint and agree with me, for a change."

An honest reply stuck in her throat, so she lifted her hands and formed a halo.

"Hey Fallon—are you coming?" An expectant smile punctuated Court's request.

The halo melted into a wave and she backtracked in a jog to get her journal and camera. The tacks shook loose from her day as she ascended the tower for her gear. The curved shoreline of the big lake flashed to mind. A cozy smugness settled onto her inner horizon, and to think it all started with a little heart hiccup. *This is a divine ripple, right God?*

~

Court scraped his shoe on the dock, waiting for the third party to join his boat parade. His teenage assistant clunked around the old man's boat, stowing loose equipment and coiling lines. A reluctant scan of his old work horse revealed nothing that could be straightened up to make a better impression on the interesting woman that kept him waiting. A bait hauler couldn't be mistaken for anything more luxurious. Better to be genuine anyway. Still, he would enjoy the company. To add purpose to his lake run made the day extraordinary in an unexpected way. The time he'd made up with the rushed lock sequence leaked back downstream until Fallon appeared in a run from the tower's base.

"All set, Liam?" he called to the youth. The kid straightened and moved behind the helm, assuming steering duty. Liam saluted a confirmation as Fallon jogged down the ramp. Court offered her a hand in which she accepted after a sudden halt. "Didn't anyone ever tell you not to run on a dock?" The tease in his voice unmistakable, she tossed off the correction with a smirk as she stepped toward him into the boat. When the hull rocked, he swayed toward her.

She tapped his chest with her record book. "I'll be conducting my monthly shoreline assessment as we go. Thank you for taking on the piloting task and allowing me to concentrate on the canal." She pushed the waterproof notebook up behind the windshield and stepped back to get the stern line.

He hid his pleasure by mirroring her efforts on the bow line, and then cranked the motor to get underway. The influence of the craft in tow became apparent as the stern muscled down into the water column to give a mule's pull to their inert shadow.

"You good, Liam?" she called.

Court spotted the teen's thumbs-up signal and ratcheted up the speed, nosing into the canal. "So what's a shiny little rainbow trout like you doing trapped on the lock?"

Her eyes glistened, though her hands reached dutifully for the notebook. "I'm fond of my work on the water."

Unconvinced that recording lake levels would be her sole focus, he headed for the most beautiful place on earth. He wouldn't push the allegiance, as the familiar scenery improved with her in his boat. His initial lock rescue now morphed into a sustained secondary resuscitation, one that made his heart beat with greater purpose.

Chapter 2

Knowing the sequence of Port Mayaca lock would be abbreviated compared to her home station, Fallon felt torn between offering Liam assistance or remaining aboard with Court to rub shoulders as a friendly duo. "Should I go back and help Liam navigate the lock?"

"Let the kid prove his merit and solo through this. He'll call for help if he needs it. Remember, he left his mother back there at the campground."

"Thanks. I needed help thinking through it. I'll take the stern line, unless you have a preference."

He laughed and regarded her with a tantalizing smile. "I've never had help before, fore or aft, so let's see what it feels like." He tipped her cap brim up and stepped forward for bow duty. "We wouldn't want to put a scratch on this baby, now would we?"

Delighted with his wit, she stepped into the stern and waited for the helper to appear topside. "Goodness no. All these lives at stake—that's some responsibility." When he shot her a quizzical look, she nodded to the bait box.

He laughed again. "My brother calls me irresponsible—ducking shop duty to make the run up here."

"Oh, where's headquarters for your bait shop then?"

"Port Salerno is where my father got his start. We have some waterfront property near the harbor in Manatee Pocket, where the river runs into Indian River Lagoon."

"I don't know that area, but it sounds charming. I've always heard that Port Salerno is old school Florida surrounded by Stuart's concrete sprawl."

"Yeah, I've got a Florida cracker cottage on Centerboard Lane that I'm trying to resuscitate one room at a time. Summer's no time for indoor work though. Plus, my brother's wife is due to deliver their third small fry by mid-June, forcing me to take on more responsibility at the shop."

"How about you? Small fry I mean…"

He shook his head dismissively and tossed his bow line up to the lock attendant who wrapped it around the cleat. "Me? I'm all bait and no catch. I trust God with that though, as he helped Peter catch fish against all odds."

She chuckled at his analogy as she recognized the man in uniform above. "Hey Andy. Here's the stern line." She hurled the coil and it landed right in his hands. Court came down behind her and took a look into the bait box riding the stern. She witnessed a banking flash of silver as he closed the lid. "Are they part of the odds against you?"

He gestured with a sweep of his wrist. "My sister says I'm a connector who spends all my time helping others instead of investing in my own life. I don't know how that might look any different."

"Well for one, you could have stayed in your boat at the lower lock and let the old man become someone else's problem, namely mine. The outcome wouldn't have been quite as hope-filled." The tower signaled the gate opening and a rush of water came at the vessel. He grabbed her arm to pull her up front. She retrieved her notebook and settled in for something she could be more certain about—flow rates.

~

Court allowed the rush of water to sooth his senses as he stole a glance while Fallon wrote. The run had an official feel to it with her aboard, which birthed an air of legitimate purpose. Maybe he could offer to bring her up the canal again if the arrangement suited her. For such a pleasurable view, he'd make it work in his favor.

The lock flooded, lending a sense of privacy. When the gate doors yielded, the horizon gave way to the glorious openness of Lake Okeechobee, spectacular despite its familiarity. He became impatient to throw off the tethering lines and enter the shimmering blue.

Fallon stood as the boat started, braced for motion. "Magnificent." Her gaze scanned the aqueous expanse stretching before them.

A flash of kinship nestled his chest as he clamped both hands on the wheel. He allowed the boat a more leisurely trajectory than usual until she pointed out a calibrated marker along the eastern shore. Duty called, so he yielded to her direction. The reading lasted long enough to irk a vagrant blue heron, and they were underway again headed north.

Jake's Fish Camp came up the shoreline off a short

dock. He nosed behind the shack to lose the old man's boat. Cutting that particular tow line also severed his privacy with Fallon, but dropping Liam aboard wouldn't change everything. Maybe the teen would make a good route runner to replace him when he had to anchor the bait store. He gave it some thought as the bow eased beside a weathered dock. When Fallon moved forward without a word to secure the line, he could scarcely look at anything else.

Liam shrugged his shoulders. "Where do you want me?"

"Drift into the rear slip after I pull in the tow line." He hustled to break the kid free.

Fallon stepped up onto the dock and motioned for a line. Liam flipped the rope and she tied his craft opposite the bait boat.

Court secured the stern and stepped out to assist with the second boat, leaving enough line for the wind to blow it off the pilings. "Good job, Liam. Here comes your next challenge, so see what you think of it."

The kid placed both feet on solid wood. "I'm ready, if you're looking for help."

"I need an assistant route runner when I have to stay at the bait shop this summer. How about I take you through the loop today as training for a part-time job?"

"Like an internship," Fallon added.

Liam scrunched his sailor's cap in his fist, his eyes widening. "I'd like a real job. Mom doesn't need me at the campground all day. I even have a boat, when she lets me use it. We could retrofit a bait box on it."

Court held up his hand to halt the enthusiastic reception. Maybe the kid just woke up to his responsibility, which he'd encourage full-throttle. "You handled that lock back at Port Mayaca like a pro, so let's get you introduced to the shop owners. Then I'll show you how to disperse the baitfish. I've brought bloodworms, too, so let's go get the order from Jake and see how we can help him today."

"Awesome, Court—or do I have to call you Mr. Court since you'd be my boss?" Liam hastened up the dock toward the shack.

"Court will do, Liam. Let's call it a partnership of sorts, since you're taking on my legwork." He rested his hand on the small of Fallon's back to encourage her to walk ahead.

"Do *I* have to call you Mr. Court?" She fired a teasing look over her shoulder as something plunked in the water beside the dock.

Her flirting tone hit him like a tickle in a tender spot. He had to swallow before he could declare a comeback. "Maybe Mr. Reynolds would be more appropriate since we've just met." That earned him a raised eyebrow as the screen door slammed shut behind Liam. The water glimmered down below, giving the ordinary shack a mystical appearance in its reflection.

~

"I'm Fallon McKenzie from the Corps office at St. Lucie Locks. It's nice to meet you, Jake." Extending her hand over the counter, the proprietor stopped rigging the lure long enough to make the exchange. "I've been stationed there less than a month, but I'm a native from Loxahatchee."

Jake cleared part of the counter with the back of his hand. "Hmm. Lots of horsey people down there from what I recollect."

Court pulled off his hat and wiped his brow,

accentuating the still air in the shop.

"Yeah, I'd be one of those, I guess. We have a horse ranch on eighty acres, more or less, if you count the swampland." She tapped her notebook on the counter. Emblazoned with the Corps official crest, a moment of business might be in order. "I'm conducting my shoreline survey today, and lucky enough to have Mr. Reynolds offer to bring me up with him."

Jake smirked. "I don't call that luck—sniffing a bait box the whole way around."

Court straightened defensively. "Hey, fish smell comes with the territory, Jake."

Fallon smoothed her notebook page. "I never even noticed. Do you have anything to tell me about conditions on the lake? Anything unusual? Oil slicks on the surface? Erosion on the banks?"

Jake made a low whistle. "The skeeters are already bad. Reckon you can do anything about that?"

"Not beyond looking for stagnant spots that might be breeding them."

"Minnows eat the wigglers in the shallow grass," Court said. "If you don't have anything else to complain about, let's get to my baitfish order. This is Liam. He might be taking my runs for awhile after my brother drops out to help tend his newborn next month."

"Okay. Where are you from, Liam? Are you a local?"

"We live in Lake Worth during off-season, but my mom's the campground manager at St. Lucie Locks all summer. I have my own boat there and can make the run here and back, no problem."

The old-timer chuckled and put the lure aside to size up the new recruit. "Where there's water, there's always trouble, young man. Keep your wits about you and always check the weather. Now come on back and I'll show you where the live bait well stays. Today I want two dozen, but Friday I'll need four because of the Memorial Day tournament."

"Let me recommend five dozen, Jake," Court replied. "I heard they have a record number of entrants, my team included."

Fallon stowed that information to offset the nagging worry that he might not be around regularly.

Jake shoved the screen door open. "Going for that big prize money, huh?"

"Somebody's going to win it, so why not a poor bait peddler?" He touched Fallon's back again as they traipsed across the narrow back deck.

She recalled his earlier comment prohibiting running. "Too fast for you—or too slow?"

He blew out a breath as Jake stooped to pull a heavy rope out of the water. Liam lent a hand as water sloshed out of vents in the side. "Just right," he replied in a private tone.

She backed against the building to let him come up beside Liam, allowing the compliment to drift through her core.

"Liam, you can fit six dozen or so in here, so put the whole order in without a worry. They'll be fine." Weathered wood planks groaned underfoot as Jake lowered the bait box, motioning them back down the dock.

The youth seemed antsy to make progress. "Come teach me how to scoop 'em out and get my count."

She held up at the shack while the lesson unfolded, noting the patient instruction that the teacher imparted.

Admiration floated to the surface as she assessed her new friend, the one who connected others without regard for himself.

"He's a good guy," Jake said through the screen, counting out money to pay for the shiner deposit. "Faithful as they come." He tapped the bills against the door frame and gave her a sharp nod.

When she grinned, it set off his secret wink like a channel buoy set on automatic blink. Her escort seemed to be a local favorite, which made her relax a little. The notebook nearly slid from her hand.

~

Had it not been for the flood control rim around the lake, Court figured he'd be able to spot the skyline of Clewiston to the west. As Fallon leaned over the gunwale to make her last reading of the day, he killed the ignition to allow the boat to drift. Enticed by the offer of a paying chore, Liam had stayed back at the last shop helping the shopkeeper prepare for the tournament. The private setting worked on him again, something he had difficulty acclimating with. He wanted to ask her a few things about her personal life, but had to get something of utmost importance out of the way first. Pretending to neaten the bow cubby, he searched for a way to pitch his concern.

She tucked the notebook behind the windshield. "Are you trying to give the kid a chance to finish up?" She tugged her shirttail out and began unbuttoning the uniform.

He kept his back turned to give her a few seconds to adjust to the late afternoon heat. He needed to think of a way to knock the hurry off their return. "It doesn't matter to me either way, as I'm punching off the clock."

He dropped the bow line in a coil and started aft.

She flexed her arms like a windmill and tone muscles danced beneath the straps of her green tank top.

"This place is a little bit like heaven on earth for me, so let's give it an extra minute since we've made it around this far." His hands swept the lake outline. "I tend to think heaven will have a glass floor that looks a lot like Lake Okeechobee." He stepped to the stern and pulled a fishing pole from an oar pocket. His fingertips tested the line. Now, he really had to go fishing because he needed to know her soul condition. Anything else would be dead in the water. "Will I see you up there someday?" He lifted the box lid, found a dead shiner floating at the top and grabbed it out.

She settled into the corner of the stern next to the bait box, gazing out over the water. "Oh, you'll see me all right," she replied, her voice steady and sure. "That'll be me standing next to Jesus, my face all shiny in reflection of his glory. I sense you're casting your nets again, Peter, but you don't have much bait."

"You're right, only a solid hunch and one dead shiner. But that might be just enough." He punched the hook through the dead fish's lip and cast out toward the grass line of the shore, easing next to her on the stern. He offered the pole and she took it, freeing him to wipe his hands. "Now bring it back nice and slow, half a crank at a time."

She responded, letting a seagull overhead hold the conversation.

Several minutes ticked by and he found contentment watching dragonflies dart along the rushes on shore.

"This is my best day at work so far," she admitted,

her arms flexing on the pole.

He placed his hand between hers to test the line, taking the indirect compliment right in the sternum. He felt the rub of a strike and the pole's tip nosed down ever so slightly. "Glad I could be part of it." He released the pole and leaned away as a precautionary measure. "Maybe you could tell me about your horse ranch in the swamp."

She started to laugh, but let it fall short as her arms brought the pole up in a jerk to set the hook. "I believe we may have caught a fish, lock runner."

Before the pole dipped out of her hands, he clasped it and bumped shoulders while she cranked the reel. A familiar adrenalin rush fueled the rest as they worked together. He clamped one hand on the net once the bass glinted in the shallows and hoisted it into the boat.

The fish objected to his grasp in a slickened twitch, but he maintained control until the bass plunked into the storage unit. "Welcome to Bait Crate." Turning back toward his guest, he raised a flattened palm for a high five, but she'd already launched a shoulder hug that shattered his good buddy move into a thousand pieces. Her hair smelled like rain as he tucked into her neck. A bad case of sea legs came on him next. If not for her holding him in place, he might have fallen right out of the boat.

"Best day ever," she repeated, pulling away with twin dimples showing.

He released her to the far side of the stern, but not because he wanted to. They couldn't stay wrapped up like that for no reason out here in the great wide open. A horn sounded, drawing the canal to mind.

"How about going to Clewiston with me Friday

night for the catfish special at Martin's Marina? I could drive the bait up to your lock station and have Liam run the route in his own boat, saving me the mileage."

"But you're fishing the tournament the next day, remember? I don't want to keep you out late the night before."

He bent down to stick the net back into the side cubby and brought his most charming smile up when he resurfaced. "Who is this woman saying 'no' to catfish?" He made it seem unfathomable.

She laughed and soon held her hands up in surrender. "Well, when you put it like that, I mean yes, I'd be delighted."

Court put his foot on the cooler lid to still his quaking knees. Life had ratcheted up a notch, for sure. Now, Friday couldn't come soon enough.

Chapter 3

Arriving by car seemed like cheating to her as most of the patrons tied up at the marina's dock. Fallon sensed that more than summer kicked off tonight. Memorial weekend launched with sunset. For once, she could be found among those celebrating.

Court touched her shoulder blade and pointed to the brown pelicans perched atop the pilings like a postcard. The smell of fried onions wafted on the breeze. "Let's come down to the docks after dinner and check out the boats. I'm starving, but I think we've managed to beat the Friday night crowd." Dressed in an aqua polo shirt and khaki cargo shorts, he reached for the restaurant's door.

She stopped to study the nautical decor. "At long last we're getting around to the best attribute of fish. How they taste certainly helps us put up with how they smell." She tossed him a playful look.

He tucked his sunglasses into his shirt. "Isn't that the truth?" Squinting into the dim interior, he searched for the absentee hostess.

"Friday night, all you can eat catfish," she read from the laminated menu at the register. "Are you going to try to amaze me tonight with how much catfish you can ingest?" She pumped her brows for emphasis.

He chuckled. "Stop me if I get carried away. I give you permission." A red-haired middle-aged woman appeared looking too weary for the early dinner hour. "Table for two please. Out of the way, if you've got one."

"I've got one off the back dock if you don't mind the setting sun."

Fallon stepped in front of Court. "That sounds perfect." When his fingertips stroked her back, she shivered. As they followed the hostess, the aroma of fried fish filled the room.

"If that gets to be too much fresh air, you just say so." He motioned toward the table.

She banked left to avoid facing the fishing fleet behind the restaurant. Maybe her new fisherman friend would enjoy that open water view and they could both be happy. A menu slid onto the table. Soon two waiters brought a platter out filled with golden-fried delight and began serving a table nearby.

"Let me order, if you will. I think we know what we want."

His assertion made her uneasy, as she had only begun to glimpse the sumptuous fare on the listing. He might be a regular, so did that make her his girl-of-the-week? The possibility poked a tiny hole in her expectations.

Court leaned forward. "I've never eaten here before, but Jake couldn't stop raving about the catfish, so I thought we'd better give it a try. Come along with me on this inaugural voyage into gluttony, so I don't punish myself solo."

She exhaled, relaxing at his admission. "I get it, the misery loves company routine. Two can play along with that, as long as salad bar comes with the catfish deal, or a side salad."

"I'll ask." He trapped her hand atop the menu. The slow pull towards him arrested time as he gazed into her eyes. A pendant lamp gave a soft glow between them as muffled noises echoed from the kitchen.

A waiter soon stepped into their domain. "Try our famous Friday night catfish dinner. It comes with all-you-can-eat entre, endless visits to the salad bar, and a shared dessert du jour. Tonight, skipper, that's key lime pie. I wouldn't miss it if I were you."

"Put us down for two Friday specials then—with no regrets."

The young man marked on the order pad and swept the menu off the table. "Help yourselves to the salad bar. Clean plates are on the front end."

Fallon stood away from the booth. "Where can I wash my hands?"

"Look for the door marked 'gulls' on the far wall." With a nod, he left for the kitchen.

She found a door marked 'buoys' first and shrugged her shoulders until Court hooked his thumb at the sign around the corner. "Meet you at the salad bar."

"Leave me some olives, will you?" He twitched a lopsided smile and shoved the buoy marker to leave her standing in a quiet spot with an unobstructed water view.

"Your first date?" the red-haired hostess asked,

taking an errant swipe at a crumb on a nearby tabletop.

Not intimidated by the intuitive woman, Fallon held her ground. "Are we that obvious?"

"He can't take his eyes off of you—and that's right where you want to keep him, honey."

"I'll try to remember that, Minnie," she replied, reading the woman's nametag.

"Let him have most of the pie when it comes. That'll end dinner on a sweet note."

"Yes, ma'am," Fallon replied, feeling the weathered wood of the door on her fingertips. She entered the restroom where the unsolicited advice mingled with cheap air freshener. So she had Court right where she wanted him, which came as breaking news to her.

~

"Did you relinquish the St. John's River post for the St. Lucie Locks?" Court thought her migration south seemed like a demotion. A slice of boiled egg rode a leaf of romaine lettuce into his mouth with pleasant results.

"You know what they say—if you've seen one manatee, you've seen them all." Her mouth pressed into the most beautiful shape after the teasing reply—almost like a heart.

He pushed a ripple-cut cucumber slice around to catch some creamy dressing. "The real truth centers around the locks being closer to home. Right?"

"True, I'd been watching the job postings for something a little closer to home. I missed my horse and my folks. Plus, the St. Lucie Canal locks have always fascinated me. I wanted to learn as much of the state as I could early in my career. I already have eight years of service."

"Which makes you what, twenty-eight?" He looked down with a sheepish grin.

A smile let him know his inquiry might have been expected. "Twenty-seven. How about you?"

"Twenty nine—and not holding. I'll be thirty this fall. My dad calls that the age of accountability. Like there's going to be some vast changeover at that time marker to make me more of an upstanding man in the community." They shared a laugh, which must have conjured the genie from the kitchen, as dinner appeared on a silver platter. He gave the server a moment to settle the plates and then reached for her hand. "Let me bless the food."

She placed her fingers into his. "Fine, but no 'good grief, let's eat.' Let's really mean it."

"I do," he said, his voice husky. "I mean, I will." He bowed his head and squeezed her hand in his. "What a night, dear heavenly Father. What an honor to have company. What a treat to have someone else do the cooking, and what a blessing to be served such tasty fish. May you bless it all, and keep our eyes on heaven. Amen."

She rubbed her thumb across his fingers. "That was beautiful, Court. Sorry I teased you about making it real. Oh gosh, look at me holding you up from tasting the best fish this side of the Mississippi." She unclamped her grip and fiddled with her napkin. "Guess you can tell I don't get taken out often."

He soaked her in, bashfulness and all. He'd found a genuine beauty among the utility of the locks. "It's my gain and privilege, all because you couldn't refuse a catfish dinner."

She punched her plate with a random stab of her

fork, lifted the speared specimen and circled it toward her mouth. "Now, let's see if I made the right choice."

"You made the right choice." His heart was talking too much now, so he pitched a load of crispy chunks into his mouth and chewed with satisfaction. The delight worked up from his taste buds to his brain to cast an authentic vote.

"Oh dear me. This *is* divine." When a second taste disappeared, her eyes twinkled.

"To tonight," he replied, lifting his water glass toward her in a toast.

"Tonight—when my crush on catfish first began." She touched her glass to his and dabbed at the corner of her mouth with the napkin.

"To the start of something good then." Whatever force of nature had crossed his portal, it suddenly drove his desire to change sides of the booth so he could be closer to her. "Can you see the sunset better from over there?"

"Probably, all you have is the fleet. Want to come over?" She scooted to the corner.

"Finally, we choose to work from the same side of the boat." He pushed his plate onto her placemat. When he bumped her shoulder sliding in, he earned a sideways glance.

"This may not be the most space-efficient approach."

"This late in the day, we'd better trade up for cozy. A fisherman can relax, after all, once his boat is out of the water." He downed another encrusted bite that tasted like more. Now that he had the proximity he'd wanted, he settled in for a feeding frenzy. Two plates later, the waiter slid an unnaturally green slice of key lime pie in front of him, snapping him out of a most pleasurable stupor. Checking the window, he opted for a quick transition. "Box that thing up for me, will you? Dessert is destined for the docks tonight." He tossed his napkin over his plate and leaned to retrieve his wallet, brushing Fallon's arm.

She glanced from him to the window. "I'll help cover the tip, as our server proved to be as invisible as wait staff can get. Are we chasing the sunset?"

"Yes, and I'm about as flatfooted as a sailor can get, so it won't be much of a race. Maybe that extra helping wasn't a good idea." He produced two large bills and tucked them under his plate.

"You were just showing those fish who the boss is, which should be your aim tomorrow."

"That's right." He stood and brushed his lap clear of hushpuppy crumbs. "Bass all over the lake will be sleepless tonight on account of me. Hey, did I mention? I've asked Liam to fish with Carter and me for Team Bait Crate." He took her hand and helped her out of the booth. The carryout box appeared and he took it while dashing for the front door. As he held it open for her, the hostess gave him a long wink.

"You two make those sunsets count now."

"Appreciate it, ma'am. We'll be back—next time we have something to celebrate." He stepped outside and hooked a strong left to follow Fallon down to the docks. The muted light now took the pressure off the day. Rigging tinkled against masts along the canal as sailboats waited out the night. His hand found the crook of her arm as she carried the dessert box.

"You're making Sheri's weekend by asking the boy along like that. She worries about him not having a strong male role model. Charlie's trying, but he's more like a doting grandpa."

"That's because he *is* Liam's doting grandpa, so good call." He helped her step down onto the dock as the shock in her expression gave way to understanding. "Charlie's son is the absentee father, which is why Sheri gets the campground concession every summer."

A balding man rubbed the teak wood cabin of a sailboat as they ambled by. "Evening," he said with a slight wave.

The bow line moaned against the water's movement and everything seemed in natural balance to Court. "Smart to be on the west side of the lake to avoid the holiday traffic."

"You don't get my age without learning a trick or two."

"Your wife wouldn't want to miss this sunset," Fallon said, indicating the far horizon. She stepped closer and Court maneuvered an arm around her waist.

The boater knocked twice on the cabin. "Time for sunset." He moved forward for an unobstructed view.

Court led her down the dock to an empty slip and sat braced against a piling. A brown pelican atop the post flaunted its wingspan and shuddered to adjust to the company, but didn't outright forfeit its claim. He examined their sunset roost and found it to his extreme liking.

Fallon settled next to him, sitting sideways on the planks with her ankles folded beneath her. "Great spot." She leaned out over the water to take in the sunset directly over the canal.

"Here, come closer." He dangled his leg over the dock edge and slipped half a width over to allow her a better vantage point. Within seconds, the fire-orange globe touched the water's horizon and the ageless process of melding elements began. He regretted not having his arm around her until she moved closer.

"Such a joy when those two meet every day." She broke her gaze long enough to include him in the sentiment as the sun flat-bottomed onto the immovable watery horizon.

A tide birthed inside Court with such magnetism he'd never experienced before. It had little to do with the canal or the sunset. Fallon had breathed it to life with the sound of her voice, launching a pull that created an imbalance of a different sort. As the fireball's cap succumbed to the earth's spin, he sensed a new horizon.

Moved to touch her, his fingertips landed along the curve of her jaw line. Her eyes carried the sunset back to him. When she dropped her chin, he pressed a kiss into her hairline, holding it for the seconds necessary to appease the rising force. Sunset became a crown of golden rays as they sat together. When her head came to rest on his shoulder, their merger deepened the internal buzz. Degrees of golden-orange played out against a thin cloud bank until the sky held only a violet rim.

She rubbed his arm where her head had been only moments before. "You have a tournament to win tomorrow."

"Right. We'd better head back. I guess we can share the pie in the truck." He stood and pulled her up, wrapping her in a hug before surrendering the dock to Clewiston's overnight guests. Their avian chaperone quivered its feathers in a final sendoff, leaving him to contemplate angel wings and other hushed forces that brushed at humankind during such tender moments from dockside.

Chapter 4

Though Fallon had mentioned her three days off, Court wouldn't be expecting her in the crowd. Sheri had been easy enough to convince to come along. They pulled into the park at Okeechobee to witness the weigh-ins ending the first day of the tournament. A carnival-like atmosphere had transformed the sleepy rim town where excitement catalyzed activity along the north shore. Fifty boats or more drifted toward the official platform to record their catches as men swarmed the judges' station to get the tallying done.

Sheri slammed the car door and adjusted her shirttail over her ample hips. "Goodness me, this brings back memories. My dad used to compete. It made Mom crazy at times."

Fallon exited the parking lot toward the main hub of activity. "I can see why." A man passed with large food storage tubs that now held paper trash. Her lime green sport skirt flounced with every step. She pulled her visor in place and second-guessed her reasons for wearing such a lively color. When Sheri pointed to something ahead, she veered off her intended course to follow the signal. A popular lemonade stand loomed ahead.

"Let's get a drink and take in the sideshows."

Fallon slid a ten dollar bill onto the ordering ledge. "What's your flavor?"

"Plain lemonade for me."

"We'll have one regular and one strawberry lemonade, please." Her payment vanished under the man's thin fingers. Soon two drinks appeared, stabbed with red plastic straws. She crumpled the change in her fist as she claimed her icy refreshment. Applause broke out from the tally board. She turned to discover someone had received credit for the biggest largemouth bass of the day.

"Thanks for the drink, and for rescuing me from another boring afternoon of campground life." A rare smile flashed from her friend as she turned to the lake. "Do you see Bait Crate?"

"They sit about twenty boats back. It's going to be awhile. Maybe we can wander over and catch their attention off the city dock. Let's cheer them up with a pep talk and find out how their day went."

"We can memorize the leader board and give them an update on the standings."

"Memorize nothing," she replied, drawing the smart phone out of her back pocket. "Get me close enough and I'll get a shot of the postings for them."

"Well, you'll have to surrender the phone to them," Sheri added, her tone carrying a warning. She stepped around a group of spectators and got closer. "Women aren't allowed to board the boat during a tournament.

It's considered bad luck."

"I don't believe in luck, but I'll give Court his space because he has enough helpers underfoot. Let's go see what that bass came in at, okay?" She locked an arm through Sheri's elbow and fought her way into the thick of things until the rim of the lake kept her from going another step. She centered the phone's viewfinder on the leader board, waiting for a judge to depart the premises. She took a clear shot with the zoom maxed out.

"I'll save Liam some of this lemonade. It's got a strong kick, just the way he likes it."

"I need to develop a heart for others like yours, Sheri. Maybe I've been by myself for too long. You lose your tendency to reach out when you don't get much practice." She slid the phone into her back pocket and followed her friend away from the rim.

"Something tells me you might be approaching an opportunity to practice."

"Do you mean with Court?" A stranger jostled her and she had to fall back behind Sheri which gave her time to formulate her own answer. "I think you might be onto something. I'm definitely interested. He's naturally outgoing. I hope that doesn't make us a poor match." The admission sank deeper, lending her the motivation she'd been lacking to step into new territory. Not an insignificant gain for a woman latched to a canal lock for most of the day.

"You're such a great person, Fallon. Just be generous with yourself and it'll fall into place. Wait and see. Nobody knows what's around the next bend in the canal, but you can sure paddle forward with purpose."

"Or tack into the wind if you're sailing." Boats with

tall masts at Clewiston came to mind and the thought of sitting on the dock at sunset spurred her immediate intentions. "Let's get to that city dock so we don't miss an opportunity to reach out to Bait Crate."

"You've got it, girlfriend. Ever met the brother?"

"No. All I know is that his name is Carter and his wife is about to have their third child. Court assumes shop duty in Port Salerno next month when that happens."

"Uh-oh. That might put a hurdle in your fast lane for summer romance, but I'm sure grateful for the job it created for Liam."

"We'll make it work out. Court still has to deliver the fish, after all, and who says I can't go into town once in a while?" She tried the lemonade and the strawberry pulp coated her dry throat like salve.

"See, you're reaching out already. It's instinctive if you get your head in the right place."

"Head and heart," she added, knowing parts of her psyche lagged popular society by a good decade. She'd never fawned over anyone before. It seemed a little late to be starting now, but who was she to question the provision of a generous God?

Her grandmother had always been fond of talking about everything having its proper time as they gardened together. Romance truly fell under her time-tested sentiment, even if nothing tangible existed, like a kumquat to snap off the tree. She searched for Bait Crate's boat and sipped her lemonade, trying to quell the inner excitement of reconnecting.

~

Court allowed the boat to drift by the city dock's edge.

"My mom? What's she doing out here?" Liam turned toward shore as two women waved them down off the west end. Sheri's hand shoved a drink over the gunwale and the teen leaned out to grab it.

Court tipped his hat and welcomed the lime green cooling effect. "Imagine seeing you here." He reached for the second cup offered.

"Hey there, mighty men of Bait Crate fame," Fallon replied. "That's strawberry lemonade—if you can stand the sweet."

"We've been out of drinking water for over an hour, so I could almost stomach lake water right now."

Carter shouldered over to his side of the boat without consideration. "What about me?"

Court grimaced. *So much for favorable first impressions.* "Fallon, this is my brother, Carter. He doesn't deserve a handout since he hasn't been much of a contributor to the team effort today." A water bottle made its way toward the boat for Carter. One sip of the pink lemonade revived his spirits, especially since the shore looked pretty fine from where he stood.

Fallon flashed a cell phone over the railing. "Anyone interested in a glimpse at the current leader board?"

Impetuous, Carter shot over the gunwale to gain the heads-up without hesitation.

Court pulled the boat off the dock's edge and lowered his sunglasses to leave a wink behind. Fallon clapped and pointed back at him, which launched a sensation the two knuckleheads on board couldn't touch. The weigh-in line shortened and he pulled forward. A look over his shoulder told him the women had already left, but her optic green outfit shouldn't be too hard to spot in the crowd later.

"Nobody's posted anything over ten pounds yet," Carter said.

"Nobody but us," Liam added.

Court slapped his shoulders, recognizing an ace-in-the-hole angler when he saw one. They would need every ounce in the end. Today, the competition was steep. He must be losing his touch, as the thrill seemed to diminish as the day wore long. The fish hid from everything they dangled into the water column.

At least Fallon had showed up to provide him a kick of motivation to finish strong. Change seemed inevitable, even on the lake. Considering how it had been dug by a meteorite eons ago, he didn't believe it would take another cataclysmic strike to bring the landscape into its next phase, at least for him. He daydreamed what that might look like for some time.

Finally, he throttled against the judges' platform where Carter relinquished their catch for the day. The weigh-in basket scored the scale's total. Several fish were weighed and measured individually. A final deposit into the holding tank sealed the deal. Court held his breath.

For heightened effect, the judge recorded the twelve-pound largemouth first, chalking into virgin territory on the leader board. When the audience broke into applause, Court caught a flash of lime green cavorting from the sidelines.

He needed that moment, and soon discovered he wasn't the only one. Liam rocked the boat with his boyish leaps, thrusting two arms into the clouds above as though to reach for a miracle. Looking back to the leader board, he watched the Bait Crate name placard slip into sixth place. Though in striking range, Liam had better keep jumping. They would need that miracle tomorrow.

"I'll be back in the groove on Sunday," Carter promised. "I've been distracted by Tessa's pregnancy. That's all."

"Charlie says you have to leave women plum off the boat," Liam replied. The well-placed dig didn't miss its mark as Carter wiped his face on his sleeve and tried to regain himself.

Tomorrow held a promising sheen that Court wouldn't let disappointment diminish. "That lake is full of fish yet—and I aim to take more than our share tomorrow. Rest well, as we have some catching up to do for Bait Crate's sake. They don't call it the Lord's Day for nothing, so remember to say your prayers tonight, gentlemen."

Liam's hand landed on his sun-warmed shoulder and Carter latched onto the kid to knot the team together. Far from legendary, they could at least make a blind stab at it, sport fishing being an outright gamble. He thought of Peter following Jesus' advice when his nets were empty and could commiserate after such a sketchy start. They were in the top ten, at least for now. He'd worry about the rest tomorrow. Capping his day with some lime green would take some of the sting out, so he glanced toward the ramp for a worthy distraction.

After an endless series of semi-botched attempts to trailer out by other teams, his truck dropped down the ramp. Court nosed the boat into shallow water. With the final lure dangling before him, he revved the motor and shot between the rollers. Liam clipped the winch line in place and Carter cranked the boat onto the trailer with a series of squeaks. He killed the motor and dropped back to the stern to hoist the outboard horizontal.

"Pulling up," Carter called. Liam hopped in the cab with him and the boat left the water with a feisty tug.

He shoved his knee onto the rear bench for balance and thought he saw a flash of lime green up in the parking lot. With his line of sight soon blocked by the rising truck cab, he couldn't make out Fallon's location. Still, he could hardly wait to get back to her. Hope escalating, he tapped his back pocket to make sure he had her cell phone.

The familiar splash of lake water washing out of the wheel wells lent him some comfort as they rode onto dry land, closing the separation between them. He searched the lot and recognized Sheri heading toward his truck. Two parties toted heavy red coolers beyond her. Once they cleared out, he spotted Fallon under the shade of a water oak.

Her arm flew out emphatically when a man dressed in bland colors halted her forward progress. Reading her struggle against the man in an instant, Court pitched over the side of the boat and broke into a run. Before he could get there, the jerk pulled at her sleeve and untied the frilly ends in a heavy-handed tease. Fallon pushed him back with her fists while he mocked her objection. That proved to be all the provocation Court needed. Dropping his shoulder, he lunged between them, knocking the man out of the shade and hooking a protective arm around Fallon.

"Are you okay?" he asked, searching her tear-rimmed eyes.

She nodded which sent the tears spilling.

He turned to assess the culprit who'd caused them and recognized the scoundrel. "Kit Rawlings? That's your idea of fish and wildlife protection, preying on helpless women?"

"Who asked you to butt in, bait boy?" He buttoned the shirt pocket on his uniform as though he'd been conducting a routine permit check. "Thought I'd get to know our newest lock keeper better, that's all. Right, sugar?"

Bile rose in the back of his throat as his right hand tightened into a fist.

Fallon slid her hand over his, pulling it against her hip. "Like I told you last week, Officer Rawlings. I'm only interested in maintaining a professional decorum with you—and I mean it."

He glanced back at her and her cheeks had turned purple-red under her freckles. When her top lip pulled thin, he could tell she was stewing mad. Loosening his fist, he cupped the small of her back and motioned her toward his truck. Nimble-footed, she fell in step with him and they left the sun-wrinkled warden polishing his credentials by his lonesome.

"You wouldn't want to lose that resident fish dealer's license, would you, bait boy?" Rawlings called to him.

Court paused, pivoting to look at his adversary. "This isn't about pulling rank now, is it?" He bit back the surly name that wanted to exit his lips.

The man shifted his stance like setting to withstand a blow. "Just what do you think this *is* about shell-cracker?" A smile crept up his face.

"With God as my witness, I believe this is about preference, Mr. Rawlings. The lady has expressed a preference for her company and it's clearly not *you*." When Fallon gasped, he pulled her back to his leeward side, lest any mud be slung in her direction. He led her to the truck without a word, but noticed her tears had been replaced by something much more complex.

Her gray eyes tried to hide the hurt, but she wasn't much of a poker player. She stared at the ground. "Court, I need a moment before I face the others."

"Okay, how about hopping in the truck? We'll finish with the boat prep and be ready to roll in a few." He opened the passenger-side door and lifted her onto the seat, taking a swipe at the end of her nose with his knuckle to lighten the mood. The corners of her mouth flinched in a fractured smile attempt. He balanced her cell phone on her knee and she reclaimed it with a thankful look. Temples pulsing, he dropped back to the trailer to find most of the follow-up work already had been done.

Sheri gave him a worried look. "Kit Rawlings cut in on us and I opted to give them some space. Sorry if that didn't work out like it should have. He's been a real nuisance ever since his wife left him last summer."

"Too bad Fallon has to be exposed to that in her line of work," he replied, yanking a strap tight. He gave her a weak wink and took an armload of life jackets from Liam. Stowing them in the truck's tool box, he slammed the lid and looked at his brother for an update before departure.

"I know you've got friends here, Court, but Tessa told me to get home ASAP or this would be my last tournament."

Court arched his brow back in response and gave the trailer hitch a testy kick. "Guess we know who wears the chest waders at your house. I'll see if the kid wants to ride back with them and save us half an hour, for

Tessa's sake. After all, I want the mother of my favorite niece and nephew to stay in good humor."

Liam tucked his thumbs into his tank top straps. "Yeah, mom says I can ride with them—but don't forget who landed the big fish today to save the team."

A red protest glared back, one that Court needed to address. "Get some aloe on those shoulders tonight, Lunker Liam. Or you'll be paying the piper tomorrow, for certain."

Sheri gave him a thumbs-up and walked over to the passenger door. "I thought Fallon was in here." A question rode her tone.

He glanced in the cab and it sat empty, robbing his last ounce of joy. "She must be getting the car cooled down. Could you ask if she'd be willing to come back out tomorrow for the final weigh-in? It'd mean a lot to me."

"Sure thing, Court. I'll give it my best shot."

"I'll talk it up, too," Liam added. "She won't be able to resist my boyish enthusiasm. That's what teammates are for, right?"

"And for increasing our likelihood of snagging the big ones," he replied, cutting a sharp look at Carter.

His brother flinched. "Tomorrow's my day."

Court shot a finger at Liam and fell into the driver's seat like a waterlogged floatation device. He released the parking brake with a grimace

Carter got in and slammed the door. "What's with you, big brother?"

"Rawlings made a move on Fallon over there under the oak and I had to step between them without knocking his lights out. Is that what chivalry feels like, a fillet knife in the gut?"

Carter glanced at him and dropped his chin to his chest. "I'm afraid to tell you it only cuts deeper as time travels on."

"What's that supposed to mean? I've been out in the sun way too long today to figure out your half-baked riddles." He pulled the rig out onto the open road as Okeechobee fell into his rearview mirror. Recognizing Fallon's car, he sped up to ride tandem with her until the car turned south toward the locks.

Carter cleared his throat and looked out the window for several long minutes. The lake dam blocked the late afternoon sun as they rode into its shadow. "Tessa wants to separate. The baby was my idea, to mend the rift between us, but it doesn't seem to be working. I still pray to God every night that it would. Simple-minded me."

The truth hit home like a belly-flop. All Court could do was let out a spent breath. Maybe this is how love came and went, in tears and tirades. "She's your wife for a lifetime in God's eyes. I signed that paperwork the day you married her."

"If only she could look beyond all my imperfections, I might have a chance."

"Now that's a tall order, brother-of-mine."

Carter's stoic expression only held a second before a smirk sprouted. He launched a retaliatory punch in the arm next.

Court took it in good humor. Nothing seemed quite the same as his gaze wandered over the farm fields around Indiantown. In a no-man's land rimmed with water, he had a tiny boat to float out towards paradise. The only thing that would knock back the floodwaters of rebellious risk would be a little prayer. He had forty-five minutes to launch a stretch of open-eyed supplication, so he fired it up like a weak beggar.

~

"Court, it's Fallon. Have I called too late?" She stared at the alarm clock beyond her cup of herbal tea and wished she'd noticed the hour sooner. Restlessness must have marred her mental capacity as she brooded over the right thing to do. She held her hair back off her face as her legs began to shake. She crossed her ankles while seconds ticked past.

Sounds of him fumbling the phone came over the line. "I'm lying here like yesterday's catch left on the dock, all wide-eyed and not a wink of sleep to be had."

"It didn't feel right not saying good-bye earlier tonight. That's why I'm calling." There, she'd said it and gotten the load off her conscience. She squeezed her eyes closed.

"Listen, I'm glad you did. Seemed like the fun fell smack dab out of my day when you disappeared like that. I tried to figure out how to retrieve it."

"I'm sorry for leaving so abruptly. It wasn't about you at all. I needed to pull back and regroup. Rawlings caught me out of the blue. I'm usually not that vulnerable."

"Is that because you're typically protected by uniform and protocol on the job?"

"Okay, that's a fair assessment. It does lend me a sense of control to be out there at the locks pulling duty in my khakis, but I let my guard down at the tournament."

"Hey, you looked great to me, Fallon. I could hardly believe my eyes when I saw you standing there on the city dock. Honestly, don't let some creep like Rawlings take away the freedom of your personal space. Then he wins, right?"

"Well, we certainly can't let that happen, can we?" A smile pulled at her cheeks. "May I come back and try to redeem myself tomorrow, by any chance?" She heard him fumble the phone again and had to stifle a giggle.

"Final weigh-in starts at four o'clock. I'd be ecstatic to look for you at the city dock any time after three-thirty. Think you can make that?"

"Three-thirty then. That's when we'll get this sailboat back on even keel." It floated like a promise, healing the rift of the day. She shifted on the bed and her Bible fell against her leg, a handwritten bookmark slipping out. She fingered it and an idea surfaced for saying good-bye. "Now that our plans are set, I want to read something relaxing to help my favorite fisherman drift off to sleep. Are you game for that?"

"Hold on, let me nestle back here and get loosened up. All right, I'm ready."

"The Lord is my gatekeeper, the way always opens to me on time. He charts my passage beside gentle grasslands, and then the shimmering waters open up before me, taking my breath away. This peaceable scene restores my innermost being. His name leads me down a most righteous path. Though lifeless shadows move across the low gaps, he will not leave me to empty-handed fear. His rod of divine authority lends me comfort. He releases me to feast when those set against me are constrained to famine. He caps my head with so much favor, my blessings fill up to the high water mark. Only buoyant outcomes and pleasant mercies will shadow my wake through the locks, and I will dock along the shores of the Lord for all my days, amen."

Her heart now vulnerable, she pressed her lips together and closed her eyes, the phone cradled under her trembling chin. She heard him take a long breath and waited to see if her personalized rendition struck a chord—or missed. The bookmark fluttered onto the sheet.

"Fallon, your voice unlocks a place inside me I didn't even know existed."

"If that's a soft spot, I'll do my best to keep it protected," she whispered.

"I can't wait to see you again tomorrow."

"Then do me a favor and fish for *me*, will you?"

"I will, I promise. Good night for now—and thanks for calling. I didn't think there was any hope for this day to end well, but look how things can turn around."

"Good night, lock runner. Sweet dreams." She ended the call and clicked off the light, shuffling down into the sheet to let the quiet waters roll over her thoughts. Somewhere in the heart of Port Salerno, a fisherman would sleep more deeply tonight, which gave her the snuggest sensation in the world.

Chapter 5

By late morning, the bass seemed too spooked from the excessive boat traffic to strike anything remotely resembling a lure. Court had an idea to recoup some lost time, but he'd have to convince the rest of Team Bait Crate. He left the helm and stepped back to the stern, pretending to check the live well. Liam cranked his line in to check his bait. It hadn't even been touched. They sat dead in the water.

He shot a glance up the north bank and figured as many as two dozen boats littered the shore up that way. No use competing with that. "I had a strike on the west grass beds south of Harney Pond last Friday while waiting for Liam. A little voice keeps telling me to skedaddle over there. All it would cost us is gas and time at this point. What do you say, Carter?"

"Gotta be better than this hole." His brother cranked in his line.

"I'm for it, too," Liam added. "Charlie claims we have to make our own luck, so I say let's run for it." He laid his pole in the boat and shoved some loose tackle into the pocket. "Can this old tub move out?"

"Don't judge a boat by its peeling stripes, Junior," Court replied, stepping to take the helm again. Liam came forward with him as Carter worked to catch up. The teen rolled cuffs onto his long sleeves and Court spotted his tricked-out watch. "How about timing us so we can weigh that against our foolishness later?"

"You've got it, captain. Let me get the stopwatch function going."

Court ramped up the speed. Within seconds, the boat planed toward their new destination. Carter joined them behind the console, slapping an arm over the teen's shoulders which generated a whelp over the mechanical whine of the motor. When Carter's cap went airborne, the quick-moving youth trapped it against the windshield and handed it back.

Court counted the boats they passed and kept news of his empty cooler to himself. They needed some un-company, and a place where boat props hadn't churned up the water column—a place where the bass were still hungry. The grass band grew wider to the west and he surveyed the surface ripples to pick his comeback spot.

Liam started to speak about the time the boat leveled out. Court pressed a finger to his lips, demanding silence. Carter crept back to get his pole rigged, taking a lively shiner from the bait tank. He'd no more than dropped it three yards from the boat when the pole tipped down and redemption swam up from below. Court cast his line off the stern next while Liam manned the net. Carter flashed him a look and he understood it thoroughly. Now they were fishing, and they had the untapped spot all to themselves.

~

The crowd swelled for the tournament culmination, so Fallon convinced Sheri to migrate to the city dock early. Though her haste soon came rewarded with a front rail view of the competitors' boats passing, her snapshot of the leader board had been somewhat shortchanged. An early boat posted a fourteen pound largemouth, moving that proud team into the upper slot. She scanned the jumbled weigh-in line searching for Bait Crate. Sheri pointed to a tangle of vessels where the familiar blue and red-striped bow bobbed into sight. She lowered the cooler holding the extra lemonades and secured it between her ankles.

Sheri shielded her eyes from the sun. "Hope Liam's making a strong showing for his debut tournament." She propped her elbow on the rail and took a long sip from her drink.

"I see how fishing gets in their blood. Catching a finicky creature has an instinctive guesswork to it, like you have to outsmart them. Place the refraction of the water's surface between you and your target, then the whole thing gets a little tricky."

"Give me good old terra firma," Sheri joked. "I've disliked boats ever since I was a girl."

"A boat is a getaway float if I ever saw one. Still, sometimes it helps to leave the shore and cast your cares on still waters."

"Not that my cares as a single parent could ever float away."

"Sheri, you're making a worthwhile investment in Liam. Look at him stepping up to work two jobs this summer, and pretty responsible ones at that." She watched as her assessment seemed to take some weight off the conversation.

Her guest sighed and looked back out over the lake. "It still feels like only part of a life."

"Christ died so we could have a full life, not a half-life or a shelf life, but an abundant-for-the-moment and chock-full-of-meaning-each-second kind of life." She took a drink and studied the boat movement.

"I used to believe that, but something happened inside of me and I stopped trusting God. A busted marriage can do that, bankrupt your trust. I never seemed to fully recover."

"We should make a pact as two strong women—to live life to its fullest, as unto the Lord. I hereby challenge you. What do you say?" Fallon looked over her sunglasses as her friend seemed to struggle with stepping up. "Live, laugh, and love. What's there to lose?"

"Oh, all right. We start the moment that boatload of hopeful fishermen connect with us on this dock, okay?" Sheri squared around to the rail as though to assess how long she had to end her commiseration and start anew.

"Everything starts with that boatload," she agreed, a stitch of excitement tacking the proclamation in place on her heart.

When the Bait Crate boat drifted over half a width, Liam threw an arm up to signal the start of something extraordinary. "There's my work-in-progress," Sheri said.

"Mine, too."

"Team Bait Crate here, reporting in from the top of the world," Liam called. His other arm floated up like he was celebrating the weigh-in early.

Fallon climbed the rail to get closer. "Does that mean you're heavy with fish?"

"Big fish," Court replied. An exaggerated smile hinted at his expectations.

Remembering the cooler, she slipped down the rail and produced it for Liam's grab. Sheri tugged at her waistband when she stretched to make the connection. As Liam snagged it and settled back in the boat, Carter appeared over the side, his hand extended without a word. She popped the cell phone out and cued it up, handing it over. "Fourteen pounder for the first place team."

"Gonna be tight then," Carter replied, squinting into the screen.

"Things might have changed drastically up there. We were a bit earlier today because we wanted to be down here front and center."

The boat drifted past and the captain gave her a long look with a treble-hook smile. "I appreciate that, Ms. McKenzie. More than you know."

"Go make your high mark on this fishing tournament and we'll see you in downtown Okeechobee."

Sheri joined her up on the railing, her fist swirling through the air. "Go Team Bait Crate!" Her cheerleader vigor caused Liam's arms to claim the clouds again. "I think I'm going to like this challenge, Fallon. And I plan to make the transition to full speed right out loud."

"Mine might sound a little more subtle on the outside, but inside I'm screaming right along with you, my friend." A compatriot's hug choked her as they came back to solid ground.

"Race you to the judge's platform."

"Why, you wouldn't dare." She'd barely spoken the words when her guest hitched up her flowing skirt and darted through the crowd at a trot to make good on her challenge. Not to be caught flatfooted when bigger fish were heading for the balance, she shoved through right behind her, laughing as she ran.

~

The glitter-spackled bass boat ahead of them pulled off the weigh-in platform after their name placard rattled against the planks out of contention. Court knew Bait Crate wouldn't be discarded like that, as today's redemption swam in his live well gulping air. He didn't know how far up the standings they would float compared to other teams.

Carter's face worked up an animated grin as he grabbed a dock cleat and held them on for the weigh-in. A judge with sunburned arms handed them a tub and Liam threw open the live well.

Court netted the first two fish into the test bucket. "No foul hook, just five perfect specimens of largemouth bass, fresh from God's spawning grounds into your hands." His comment cracked half a smile on the old-timer's face as they made the exchange. Not that he was trying to bilk any favor out of the man, as he'd already received his favor, earlier there on the west side of the lake. Carter passed him a second tub with exuberance and two men came alongside to retrieve it. Court took that as a positive sign their load held more weight than most.

A ripple flipped his stomach when he remembered Fallon would be meeting him in a few minutes. Something cottony pulled over his edginess and he relaxed with an exhalation, wiping his hands on his cargo shorts. This would certainly be a tournament to remember, where everything that seemed ready to fall apart suddenly came together for something beautiful.

He searched for her on the shoreline and caught a sliver of royal blue beside a floppy hat.

Now attuned to the judges, Court noted that each fish had been individually weighed and measured. When the last one made it into the holding tank, the men huddled to come to their determination. Carter bumped his shoulder, but he couldn't break eye contact with the scene up on the platform. The junior assistant took a protracted instruction from the senior judge and all the placards shifted down the display one by one until there was only one left—the team with the fourteen pounder. The Bate Crate placard came into the teen's grip and got leveled right under the top spot. They'd just landed second place.

A heady sensation came over him about the same time a whistling catcall came from shore, leading a rousing round of impromptu applause. Court tried to find Fallon as a celebratory slap from his brother landed across his back. Liam scampered onto the bow sprit to make like King Kong, chest thumps and all. The kid hollered like a Seminole warrior, and even the judges gave a few claps for the surge of fishing prowess. This time when his gaze sought deep blue, he found it waving wildly above the floppy hat. Fallon must have perched atop Sheri's shoulders. A sudden urge to swim to shore overtook him, but his brother shook it out with his repetitive back-slapping reaction.

"Now we just have to hold in place," Carter said, his lips twitching with excitement. A judge motioned for a break and he shoved off the platform, dusting his hands off. They idled up toward the ramp, exchanging handshakes as the ranking set the mood, now that they had landed in the reward zone, hot and heavy.

Court turned east and cut their speed. "Say, Liam. What are you planning to do with your part of the prize money?"

"I try to save most of my extra money, as I've got a big job that needs to be done." The boy leaned over and shined an accentuated smile at them, his meaning becoming too apparent.

Court popped the truck keys out of the hatch and handed the floating fob to Carter. "Braces are a good investment that pays off in the long run, despite the inconvenience for twenty-four months. Hey, if you're serious, I can get you a good deal from an orthodontist buddy of mine up in Stuart."

"Oh, here we go. Mr. Connector strikes again," Carter replied, grimacing as he timed his jump to the ramp dock.

"I need to get this metal-mouth party started. Talk to my mom, will you?"

"Sure thing buddy. Just say a prayer that money doesn't slip out from under our deck shoes, okay?" He laughed to reset the high mood and the teen took off his cap, leaving his hair a prime target for razzing. Being the captain in command, it was the least Court could do.

~

Fallon stood next to Sheri who had Liam on a short leash ever since the microphone cued up from the judges' platform. All Court's hugs were turning her into cotton candy on the inside. Her skin tingled where his hand rested. Off his far shoulder, Carter squirmed while waiting for the news. For a Sunday, the day had a restless unease, heightened by the press of the crowd. Waiting had never crept onto her favorites list, and the pandemonium on the platform didn't help matters much. The leader board assistant took all the competitors' name placards down and turned the entire sign toward the grandstand on shore.

"We at USA Bass would like to thank everybody for coming out to The Fishing Capital of the World today in support of these fine fishermen."

Fallon joined in with the polite round of applause that followed, glancing up to get a read on Court. Squint lines creased his tanned face as he looked out onto the lake's blue tranquility beyond the platform. She placed her arm around his waist and he gave her a quick wink.

"Come on," Sheri murmured, her feet antsy. She rolled her eyes as the tallying came to its official conclusion in the grip of the scorekeeper at the speaker's side.

"We have the final tally coming hot out of the fryer, so we'll read out all the teams in the money, starting with seventh place." A murmur swam through the crowd followed by an agreeable hush.

Two days of trolling now came down to this list. Fallon's ears itched to hear the results. The scorekeeper handed a tally page to the speaker. "In seventh place, with a purse of one hundred and fifty dollars, is Team Eel-ectricity out of Kissimmee, Florida." When a plank hastily dropped into place, a trio of old men crossed to the platform under generous applause.

"One down, five to go," Carter said, leaning past Court to convey his countdown message. Carter's bottom lip twitched with the delivery.

"In sixth place, for three hundred dollars, is Team Bad Bass out of Boca Raton."

"Mouth of the rat," Sheri said, making Liam laugh.

"You can't even go out for dinner in Boca for three hundred." She held up an open palm so Fallon clapped against it to join the applause. Three skinny surfer boys walked the plank to get credit for placing.

Carter held up four fingers and Court topped them with his hat. Glad for the acquisition, he smiled and put it on his own head.

"Fifth place, taking home nine hundred dollars, is Team Count Me In from West Palm Beach." Some back-slapping broke out behind Sheri. The winners left the stands and whooped their way to the platform in good spirits.

Carter flashed three fingers.

"In fourth place, earning a commendable one thousand dollars, is Team Cruising Speed out of Tallahassee."

When applause broke out, Court's side began to tremble. She gave him a little hug and mouthed "it's okay" to tether him to the moment—and to her.

Carter held up two fingers in each hand, swiping them across both eyes. Then he led Liam in a catty dance gyration despite the tight quarters.

"I'm about to explode on the inside," Sheri said. "Is this what living life full-tilt is like—standing on the rim of Mount Vesuvius?"

Fallon twisted toward her challenge partner with a laugh at her analogy. When Court's hand slipped off her hip to wipe his face, she missed it right away.

"Now the stakes get a little deeper, gentlemen," the announcer said.

Carter's arms flew to his teammates' shoulders, braced for slippage and a possible direct hit of a lesser jackpot. Unfamiliar with the escalation of prize money, the consideration made Fallon dizzy.

"For third place and five thousand dollars, USA Bass is proud to announce that Team That's A Fact Jack out of Jacksonville takes the prize." The crowd grew rowdy, shouting up the shoreline and giving an authentic whoop-up.

Carter's head hung in anticipation, but his hands fidgeted at his teammates to give his nervous energy an outlet. Court's trunk quaked like a tanker passing through the Panama Canal. Fallon no longer trusted the air as her lungs refused to draw a breath.

"For second place in today's tournament, with a prize bag of eight thousand dollars, is a team of more local origin I'd proud to say—Team Bait Crate of Port Salerno!"

The breath Fallon needed came as a gasp when the familiar name crackled from the microphone. Sheri jumped up and down, her hands leveraging against her left shoulder while to her right, a winning pack of back-slapping, lake-scented fishermen celebrated like savages.

The speaker laughed into the microphone. "Let's get those boys up here, can we?"

Sheri pulled her toward the plank amid the chaos and she locked Court's elbow to pass the motion along. The next thing Fallon knew, she'd been lifted off her feet and twirled around for a three-sixty spin of sheer joy above the crowd.

She came down breathless against Court's landscape and the crowd's pulse tamped back, leaving just the two of them to commemorate the moment, touch by touch. Aware of little more than his chin stubble at this proximity, she swept closer and his lips celebrated on hers. Rich beyond a hug's embrace, his gesture insisted on her full investment, paying a prize purse all its own. She trembled as Court's arms lingered long enough to set her down with care.

Sheri cleared the way as the team members finally found the plank and strode across it to the local heroes' welcome. She locked arms with her friend and the two of them jumped up and down like teenagers, awash in life-in-the-full and the splash of triumph. On the platform, Court handed Liam the second place trophy which went sky-high on contact. Fallon reached up and tried to touch the same clouds.

"I like the feel of this alive thing," Sheri said, happy tears running down her cheeks.

"Me, too." Fallon watched Court clasp hands with Carter over Liam's trophy grip. "Thank you, God, for little things like second place." The next announcement came forth for the grand prize winner, but she barely heard a word of it.

Chapter 6

Court held the backdoor open with his foot as two of the neighborhood children tried to run past him for some unknown destination inside his house. Every chair he owned had already been taken down to the street's end for the traditional holiday cookout. The cooler in his hands made like dead weight as a wasp entered above his head.

His father gave the grill a scrape-down with a worn wire brush. "You got the fish ready?"

Court made the trip shorter by resting the cooler on the back steps. His picnic table levitated in the hands of four strapping teenagers and started out the gate.

"Go vertical with that," he yelled, trying to be heard over the raucous game of croquet going on out front. It took the kids several attempts to redistribute the weight, but they finally disappeared through the narrow portal. "I'm just getting started, Dad. We stayed out an hour longer than we should have, but I wanted to catch enough fish to go around."

"I've got my fillet knife out in the car. Let me go get

it and I'll pitch in until we get caught up. Is Carter coming early?" He hooked the brush back on the grill and dusted his hands.

"He and Tessa are working through some tough things right now, Dad. I wouldn't expect him to be too early. I let them off easy this year. They're only bringing chips, so if they get here a little late, it's no big deal." He popped the lid off the cooler and enjoyed his father assessment of his haul.

"Not bad for a Port Salerno runt," he said, scratching at one graying sideburn. "Carter may have jumped the gun a bit, marrying so young. I'll ask Granny to be extra sweet with the kids when they get here. Let's see if that'll help."

"We can only ease the pressure and pray like crazy for the rest. Some of that's on Carter, in my opinion. Since I've never progressed past going steady, I'm a rookie spectator."

"I heard Carter telling Liv about your new lady friend over at the locks."

"Fallon's coming today—in about an hour. Hope she's ready for this kind of intense interaction. She lives in the sticks, so this might be overload." He grabbed the tail of his first fish as his father chuckled his way out of the backyard. Scales flew everywhere as he got the cleaning underway, his hands working on automatic while his thoughts strayed to strawberry blonde. By the time the second fillet plunked into the tub of ice water, repeated thuds echoed from his kitchen window. "Who's in there making such a racket?"

"Only me, Court-meister. I'm swatting a wasp up by your ceiling fan."

"Get down before you break something, Audie." A

final pop pressed on a nerve, but the girl soon appeared out the back door and stood barefoot, looking at him. A spray of fish scales let loose, sticking to his forearms. Her scanty attire proved the next thing to rake his ire. "Thank you for getting off my table. Now, have we talked about you covering up for modesty's sake?"

"But it's hot and it's summer," she replied. Her dirty nails dug under the red bathing suit strap to adjust it.

"You're not a little girl any more, Audie. Remember what we talked about? Keep it covered up and innocent. Now go home and get on a T-shirt, then you can help out. I have a new friend coming out today and I'd appreciate you making her feel welcome. Can I count on my favorite neighbor to do that for me?" He flipped the fish and scraped its hull, burying the knife behind the gill slit to carve out the fillet.

"Count on me, sure. I'll be the roasting hot kid who tries to please everybody."

"How's your mother's pot of beans coming? Tell her I'm checking up on her when you go in." Two more fillets slipped into the water as his father returned to the back steps. He shifted the cleaning board to center it between them. He threw a fish up on his dad's side and followed with one for himself.

Audie backpedaled toward the gate, biting her bottom lip. "She's already opened two gigantic cans of beans and dumped in some mustard. I think they'll turn out all right."

"Taste them for me, Audie. She gets distracted and lets the beans turn a little sour. Maybe add some brown sugar or something."

"Right-oh, Captain Reynolds. Permission to go ashore now, sir."

He looked up in time to catch her saucy salute. He flapped the fish at her and she took off on her mission.

His father grunted and handed him twin fillets. "Things any better over there?"

"No. Still more neglect going on than you can shake a stick at. I poke my nose in more than I should, but I can't let Deidra ruin those kids. Audie's about grown up right in front of my eyes." He tossed his fillets into the tub and his father soon handed him two more. Aiming for efficiency, he scooted the tub in the center where they both could reach. More scales went flying. Two teens from down the street came and wheeled the grill out.

"It seems like we've been trying to save pieces of this neighborhood for over fifty years. Things have changed since I grew up here, that's for sure. I remember being relieved when Tessa talked Carter into buying a house somewhere else."

"You can make a house a home anywhere, Dad. It just takes a little of this." He tapped his chest with the butt of his knife and got sprayed with fish scales in the process. Thinking he should do more cleaning and fewer orations, he sank the knife in the even flesh and let his mind wander to Fallon. This neighborhood picnic was liable to be a three-ringed circus to her, but at least the food would be good. Fresh-caught fish from Indian River Lagoon should prove enough to win her over.

"Uh-uh-uh. I do believe I'm having snook for dinner tonight, unless I mistake it for this red snapper at the last second," his father said. "Make sure none of this quality stuff gets wasted on those clueless kids."

"You've got it, Dad. I'll put a claim tag on a couple

or three just for you and Mom. How about that?" He pulled a torpedo-shaped snook out and ran the knife blade over it in admiration. Two more small fillets hit the water.

"Can I tell you outright how proud I am of your bass tournament finish? You showed those big-money boys what a real fisherman can do without all the fancy-schmancy gear."

"Give me a silver shiner with a little quiver left in it and the wind in the right direction anytime. The teenager tagging along with us sure got fishing fever right quick. His name is Liam. I'm hiring him to run the Lake O bait route while Carter takes off for the new baby."

"I thought you wanted to run the locks. Isn't that where your new gal is?"

"Yeah, well. We'll have to figure that one out, Dad. The highway and the canal run both ways. Besides, Carter will return to the shop before long and summer will be the same crazy frenzy we've always known." That earned a sympathetic laugh as he cleaned the snook and nestled the fillets vertical against the tub's side.

"Ta-da," Audie said, twirling into the back yard with a yellow T-shirt on. "It's time for some magic." When she finally stopped spinning, she pointed to Tinker Bell up by her shoulder. Even though the shirt looked a size too small, at least she seemed more presentable. She'd also pulled her hair back.

"Much better. Can you roll the cooler back here so we can load these fillets on ice?"

"Yes sir, captain. Tink at your service—at least for now." She flashed him a "showed you" smile and departed out of the gate. Maybe he could have told her to look behind the truck, but this way it seemed more like a scavenger hunt.

Three sets of fillets stacked into the tub before he realized Audie hadn't gotten back with the cooler. When he finally heard a set of wheels coming through the gate, he didn't bother to look up. His dad made an effort to straighten his bent back and dropped his knife into the fish cooler. Passing his knife along the backbone to get a healthy fillet, Court almost missed his father's throaty signal. The bony elbow, however, he received loud and clear.

"Am I in the right place for the fish dinner?" Fallon asked, standing by the gate. Her flowing hot pink outfit swished at her knees as she pulled a blue and white cooler. Her smile morphed into a questioning lip-tuck as Court stood motionless.

"I'm Jim Reynolds and yes, you're in the right place. I'm betting you're Fallon. Is that right?" He wiped his hands on a kitchen towel dangling from Court's side and stepped over to extend his hand. "Sorry, everything about this family seems to smell like fish."

"Glad to meet you Mr. Reynolds, and I don't mind the fish smell. Anybody working on the water had better be plenty used to it."

"Evidently, my firstborn son has turned into a mime all of a sudden. How about I leave you two alone for a few minutes and go try to find my wife?" He stepped around her and shot Court a corrective look as he escaped the backyard in a hurry.

Fallon released the cooler handle and pressed her fingertips together. "I know I'm early."

He could only stare as he dropped the fillet knife.

Maybe touching her would make her seem more real. "And you've absolutely made my day. You look almost too good to be hanging with the likes of me." He shoved his hands up in the air to emphasize his point. Several fish scales went flying into oblivion.

"But you're the reason I've come all this way." Her eyes shined lake blue as they stood in the shade of the pine. "Plus the promise of some out-of-this-world grilled fish."

"I'm putting some aside for those of us with discerning taste buds. Mom will fry some fish for the kids—and drop in a hundred hushpuppies to keep us fat and happy."

"Sounds great. Let me leave this coleslaw right here in the shade and come help you clean the fish since you seem a little behind." She stepped into his father's station, but hesitated to pick up his knife.

"Wait. We need to get you an apron or something to keep this from happening to you." He crossed his forearms and rubbed them together to shed some of the scales before lunging inside to get the remedy. When he came back out, she was giving his roofline the once-over. "It's humble, but it's home. Here's the best I could do." He lifted a loop over her head and pulled the apron strings around her, nudging her toward him ever so slightly. Her hands rested on the caps of his shoulders as he tied the knot. The contact made him wish the fish were already cleaned.

"Here's the bloody cooler," Audie said without looking up. Her hand flew to her mouth as Fallon stepped back toward the cleaning station.

Court called forth every ounce of patience he possessed and motioned the girl over for introductions.

He took the cooler handle and rapped his knuckles across her parted hair. "Fallon McKenzie, this is Audie Baines, my next-door neighbor."

"Nice to meet you today, Audie. And thanks for being a helper. Not too many older kids stuck around to pitch in, from what I've seen."

"Most of the guys are at the end of the street, but Court needed my help, so here I am." She tugged a few stray hairs behind her ear and twitched her nose to one side. "Looks like I might be freed up since you're here. I'd like to go wading for minnows and try to cool off a bit."

"Okay Tink. You're free to move about the water's edge. But no deep stuff unless somebody else is out swimming. Buddy up either way."

"When's Carter getting here? I want to play with Nikki."

"Within the hour. Now skedaddle and go have fun. I'll send the kids down the minute they get here, so watch for them. They're little tykes, you know."

"Yeah, yeah. I'll be on the watch-out, no problem. See you down at the end of the street when it's time to eat, Fallon."

"Count on it. I wouldn't want to miss Court's cooking, after all." She waved as the girl left the yard and hesitated, hands spread over the batch of fish.

"How about transferring these fillets onto the ice before you get scales on you?"

"Let me go wash my hands first. And grab a cleaner towel for us to use." She flew up the steps and disappeared inside.

He could soon hear the water running through the window over the sink. "I haven't remodeled in there yet, but the living room is done if you want to peek." He'd barely finished the invitation when she reappeared.

"Take me around later when we have more time," she insisted, dropping her fingers into the fillet stack.

He tugged the cooler open and the crystal ice welcomed the pink fish flesh a handful at a time. Finding the tea towel she'd brought out, he plucked out the old one and replaced it. "I'm going to like tag-teaming with you a whole lot more than Dad, even if he's faster with the knife." He tossed in a magnetic grin to make sure she knew it was a compliment.

"You haven't seen my fish-cleaning skills yet," she replied, her tone teasing. A rooster-tail of fish scales erupted from her side of the cleaning board. "How sad to be prejudged and mistaken for another pretty face." Before he could look over to gauge her sincerity, she already had the knife shimmied up the fish's backbone. The fillet soon broke free and clear.

"Holy crab cakes. She can carve a fish like butter. Be still my heart. I may have had a glimpse of heaven."

"How about a taste of heaven?" She flipped her fish like she was all business.

At first he thought she meant raw seafood, but he caught the twinkle in her eye as her face swept up to his. He hooked his index finger through her apron loop to hold her near as their lips met for an amicable reunion. The pleasure shot through him as the scent of rain made the fish smell go away. Far away. "I think we might have just taken a time penalty." He tried to resume duty, but the pleasant distraction had him in limbo.

"Speed kills. Better to be safe and slow. I might have

to invoke additional penalties if I see you're all work and no play." She circled the knife tip from his general direction, then down to the fish, and in three shakes of a gull's tail, a clean fillet came off.

"By all means, penalize me as you see fit." He picked up a fish and scrubbed at the scales, wondering if his industrious days were over. When her fillet splashed into the tub, he elbowed her for being a speed critic. She wiped on the towel riding his hip and his knife had to pause from duty again.

Chapter 7

Fallon stared at the beach cruiser Court pushed up the driveway for her use. The sun lowered enough to touch his shoulder. "I should have eaten one less hushpuppy."

"No one's too stuffed for a little pedaling exercise. Besides, I really want to show you Sandsprit Park. It opens right onto Indian River Lagoon. We can stay for sunset if you want."

"Now you have my attention. Give me my faithful steed and I'm yours—to the park anyway." She laughed and took the upright handlebars from him with authority. At least the wide seat looked comfortable. She swung a leg around and settled onto the aqua rig, giving a little push to get turned around until she could get the pedal underfoot.

Court soon emerged on a black surfer bike with wide tires and cruised ahead of her. "We'll head east until the water stops us, how does that sound?"

"Like anti-sunset, but I assume you can turn us around in time." Bearing down, she caught up with him and they soon left the noise of the street party behind. A bicycle tour for two came with a cozy touch of privacy as she stole the fish provider from his people.

"My grandparents owned this house with the pink flamingo in front, but Carter inherited it and sold it later for the down payment on their house in Stuart. Dad gave him the okay, but it still seems like a breach of the family's real estate legacy."

She hoped he'd elaborate on his heritage a little. "Have the Reynolds always lived on the coast?"

"Grandpa's dad came down from Georgia around the turn of the century and landed somewhere around Manatee Pocket. I'll veer left and show you the old harbor back in there. He became a shipbuilder's mate and raised his family along the south bank. Grandpa moved up to Centerboard Land when he married and drifted into the charter fishing business. Dad saw there was money to be made in the bait shop and staked his claim on the water's edge. That's how the Bait Crate shop came about, though Dad still likes to charter fishing parties now and then." He turned left out of the neighborhood.

She pulled closer and he tried to grab her handlebars. A quick swerve denied him access. "So Carter pulls most of the duty at the shop? How's that been divided up?"

He tugged his hat brim down to block the lowering sun. "I split my time between the shop and the fish ponds where we hatch and grow the shiners. Carter's always had a black thumb when it comes to nurturing anything, so he gravitated toward the shop. Our schedule is fairly loose, which is what allows me the time to make the Lake O bait run. We do good business up that way. I'd hesitate to let it go."

"I'd hate to see that, too, especially since I'm shackled to the canal lock and my new beau is a floating transient." She sped up so she could chase that admission with a grin.

He grabbed for her shoulder. "Taken up with a gypsy, have you?" Motioning down a rickety ramp, he braked and turned into a shabby boat works that dipped down to an embayment. "This is the tip end of Manatee Pocket. Looks like the armpit of drudgery to most, but grandpa loved it down here. Adventure to be had, I guess." He stepped down on his pedal to muscle across the sandy ground toward a concrete entrance on the far side.

"This land's forgotten by time—and fiberglass," she replied, craning her neck to see the details of old boats up on wooden braces in varying stages of hull work. The holiday break seemed more authentic here, where handwork on gantries replaced computers in cubicles.

"I'll show you Mom and Dad's house next. Let's cross over." He stood on the pedal and flexed his muscular calves to power through.

Fallon dug deep and forced the cruiser up behind him one belabored push at a time. The bike cooperated with lumbering ease and only slipped gears once. "Does your sister still live with your parents?"

"Only for two more months. Did Callie show you the twinkling rock on her finger?"

"Oh, yeah. She seems over-the-moon about getting married." The road leveled out and she caught up, noting he didn't seem to share her enthusiasm. Unsteadied by his lack of interest, her front tire wobbled and found a pothole. "Isn't marriage a good thing?"

He sighed. "Ironic that she's plunging in right when Carter might be dropping out."

"Carter and Tessa?" She grabbed his handlebars. "Tell me only what you're comfortable admitting, as I'm on the outside looking in." She glanced over her sunglasses to get a better read.

"Fallon, you're not on the outside. Just by virtue of you coming today, you've poked your way inside this lunatic asylum. You need to know the players better, that's all. I only found out myself after the first day of the fishing tournament. Carter confessed he needed to get back because things were a bit strained. Seems he talked her into the pregnancy as a cure-all for what's ailing the marriage. Dad thinks they might have gotten married too young."

"Wow. I attributed her aloofness at the picnic to the lateness of her pregnancy, but maybe she doesn't want to get to know me… if she's heading out, I mean. That would be so awful for Carter. And what about those sweet kids? Oh me." The sting traveled down her spine as she considered the ramifications. "And Bait Crate?"

"Too early to tell, I guess. I've promised to keep the shop and give him time at home once the baby comes, but I don't know what kind of changes might happen beyond that. Carter's truly good with the shop, especially the customers. We might have to diversify our services if he has to come up with child support. I hate to even think about it."

"What else could you do? More fishing charters?" She slowed to match his pace.

He pointed out a low-lying house with cedar shingles where the backyard emptied into the harbor. "Here's

Mom and Dad's place—my boyhood home. Fished right out of my own backyard and didn't even need my own boat, as poor luck would have it."

"Goodness, it *is* waterfront. Maybe that could lend itself to some business venture."

"Well, I had a call come in last week that's really has me exploring the possibilities. An executive from Motorola down in Palm Beach Gardens called to ask if we offered any corporate fishing outings as a recreational event for their employees club. Something more like a fishing frolic from shore, not a charter boat. I tell you, that kind of thing really appeals to me."

"And it's such a perfect fit," she replied, excited for the idea. "You're a real people person, Court. You should go with your strengths instead of spending so much time cooped up in the shop, and you love to cook. My goodness, this seems like a natural direction for expansion. Bait Crate Fishing Frolics." She held a palm out to him and he slapped it before he veered right and brought them out of the neighborhood. Traffic was light and the bike lane offered passage up a narrow bridge. A glance over the rail revealed the upper reaches of Manatee Pocket, a thicket threaded with a tangle of dark mangrove roots.

"We'll have to stay single-file from here to the park as this route doesn't have a bike lane." He made one quick glance back and sped up as they advanced at an exhilarating clip.

The salt-heavy air came mingled with fish smells as the shabby harbor gave way to a string of updated houses with boat slips in back. The final stretch held a modern marina and a length of untouched vegetation. She took in the transition to nature's beauty while the sea breeze lifted her hair to cool her neck. A wooden sign announced the park's entrance as they cruised through the double-lane road that ended in a parking lot flanking nothing but sand.

Court braked at a cabbage palm tree near the restroom shelter. "Welcome to Sandsprit Park. Put your bike beside mine and we'll lock them together." He dismounted and fiddled with a chain looped around his seat.

"Let's evaluate this park as a site for a corporate fishing outing. It has picnic shelters, docks, and facilities. I even see some built-in grills." A carload of teenagers filtered out of the parking lot and turned on a boom box the moment they stepped into the sand.

Court shot her a squinted glance and affixed the lock, leading her away from the noisemakers. "Pros and cons list now commencing." He held up a finger. "Pro—it has lots of shoreline for the fishing."

She laughed and worked his balled fist to release several more fingers against his mild resistance. "Restrooms, picnic pavilions, and a playground – pro, pro and pro."

"Con, con, con—uncontrollable variables related to the public, like excessive noise, competition for fishing space on the dock, drinking, smoking, swearing, and littering. Plus, you can't reserve the pavilions any length of time in advance. We tried for Mom's birthday, but they only schedule reservations one week out. Put tidal fluctuations up the inlet into the equation for good fishing and it's too hit-and-miss, I'm afraid. It's a nice park, though. Let's head for the dock off the point."

"You fishermen are a finicky lot, now that I listen to

you sort things out. Maybe Lake O would hold more promise, since you'd lose the tidal factor."

"Now that's productive thinking, but a slightly longer haul for people and equipment. We might need to write some of this down when we get back to the shop. I have some maps there we could mark up. Maybe something would jump out at us if we could stand back and look at the bigger picture." He tugged at her hand and led across the open sand toward the water's edge.

A sport fishing boat hydroplaned by the park heading out the inlet for a sunset cruise. That seemed a little more private, in an expensive sort of way. She closed the distance between them. "Does everything have to radiate out from the bait shop? Is that your hub?"

"No. Not really. It's more like 400 Centerboard Lane is," he replied, giving her an impish grin. He deserved the shoulder nudge she gave him for being so selfish in his response. "That's my gas consumption epicenter anyway. The bait ponds are at dad's house and the fishing tackle stash is split between the three of us. We really need storage space, but I'm not ready to invest until we know which way we're going with the business. Looks like we're at a turning point."

"It looks like a dock to me. How fantastic. It has steps leading right down into the water. Let's go in and look for critters."

"Good thing nobody's fishing down here or your splash party would be their undoing."

"Always thinking like a fisherman, aren't you?" She pulled him close and wrinkled her nose in a tease. Shadows lengthened across the water and she tucked her sunglasses into her hair to get a better look into the shallows.

He snickered at her exuberance and let her lead down the steps. "Going in barefoot?" He waded in wearing his deck shoes.

Some trash knocked against the concrete bulkhead and made her worry about broken glass. Her leather sandals weren't designed for submerging, so she kicked them off on the step.

"Come on, Miss Must-get-wet. I'll take you out until we're sure it's clean sand. The other flank of the spit tapers off gradually from shore and will be easier for you to walk down."

"Will we come back this way or should I carry my sandals?"

"Leave them. We'll be back in a few, especially since you ate so many hushpuppies."

She resisted slapping the back she would be riding, but managed to pinch his ear as she got situated.

He waded around with careful strides and they stirred up a minnow swarm that glinted under the water's surface in collective mass movement.

Togetherness had some perks from her vantage point, like strong shoulders and an infectious appreciation for the shore. She hooked her chin over the cap of his shoulder so their cheeks brushed a couple of times as he maneuvered in the sand. Before she knew it, her calves bumped against the dock. "Are we done?"

"Nope, just heading to the beach side. There's something along that stretch I think you'll like. Plus, we have to find a magic spot to take in the sunset. We're facing east over here."

"Right. Surprises on the shore and sunset. I like this

park, lock runner, even though you voted it down for fishing frolic fun.”

“I'm having a great time, too.”

When he moved closer as though to steal a kiss, she ducked, grabbed her sandals, and ran to the far side of the park with him trailing behind. The pavilions stood abandoned and a few resident grackles challenged the nearby gulls for making the most noise. A wet stretch of sand indicated the tide had ebbed.“What kind of surprise am I looking for, Court?”

“Watch for something moving along the bottom that's harmless but not house-less.”

“Harmless yet well-housed,” she replied, holding her hair back as she searched the ankle-deep water. A tiny shell grew legs and scuttled off for deeper water. “Oh, what's that?” She fingered the escapee and up-ended it to find legs. “Do hermit crabs live here?”

“If you find one, you can find hundreds. Always put back what you take out, little girl, so you don't break the cycle of life. I'll count for you. Go ahead and search them out.”

“Fishermen always have to count,” she replied, exaggerating a wink his way. She bent and picked at the water and out came her second find in a smoother shell.

“Two helpless hermit crabs,” he teased, over-pronouncing the number like a puppet show on public television.

“Maybe I could just enjoy them where I find them.”

“There you go. Compromise is always the best route. And it might get us to our sundown spot a little sooner.” He indicated a location down the shore that jutted out into the waterway.

She placed the critters back into the warm water of

the inlet. A brown pelican flew by and she could hear its wing beats. The lighting seemed to shift by the second, making her need to close the gap between them. "Come stroll with me out here in the shallows." She beckoned him with a hand gesture.

He stood there a moment before responding. "Like I can possibly say 'no' to that," he replied, his tone intensely personal.

"You're weak whenever you're on the shore. How terrible of me to take advantage of that." She meant her confession, but didn't think he'd let her have the upper hand. Relief washed over her when he finally waded out, shielding her from the low-slung sun with his shadow. The golden light turned his eyes a mossy brown as he hovered above her.

"Somebody's making me weak, but don't let it get around." He took her hand and entwined his fingers, leading her to the point he'd shown her. He sat down in the dry sand and motioned for her beside him, but she wiggled down in front and made him draw her back closer. The wake of a boat peeled toward shore and unzipped the edge of land to signal the close of day. Wordlessly intoxicated, she leaned back onto his shoulder and watched the day surrender to dusk. His chin tucked against her hair and there they sat, enthralled together. When the fireball sizzled against the waterline, she sent up a little prayer that ended with his arms around her.

"There it is," Court whispered, his lips moving against her skin.

Held by the sensation, she kept her gaze steady until the last of the orange dome dropped out of sight.

"Sunset belongs to us," he added in velvet

afterthought.

She turned and touched his chest, angling to take his seal of agreement right on her expectant lips. When her eyes opened again, a handful of peach-colored rays had mellowed the waterway.

"Let's ride back to the bait shop before we lose the light of day. I know a shortcut that doesn't have as much traffic."

"Thank you for my park tour. It's been wonderful." She tilted her head down only to have him take her chin in his fingertips and lift her face toward his.

"You make it wonderful, Fallon." He took her into his arms and held her close, nuzzling his face into her hair which made it incredibly hard to leave.

Biking in the dark didn't sound like a balanced formula though—plus he had hinted at some planning time together. "Take me to your shop and mesmerize me with your maps."

He stood and brushed the sand off his seat, laughing. "The bait shop's only romantic in anticipation, I assure you. If it wasn't for imminent threat of darkness, we'd be taking the long way back to keep your dreams afloat."

"I'll receive it as part of my grand adventure of the day then, bobbers, bloodworms, and all." She started back toward the bike in a casual jog, which he soon eclipsed.

"No inventorying the bait," he replied over his shoulder. "That should help preserve the romance of the evening to some extent."

She darted around him and sprinted for the bikes, leaving the vacated pavilions and well-housed crabs behind her. A lightheaded sensation swarmed her, which had nothing to do with clean air and exercise. A loner in the middle of his attention, she was blessed to be chased by a down-to-earth man, a fisherman no less.

~

Court flipped the laminated sheet over and made a larger chunk of real estate appear at Fallon's request. She seemed serious about this planning session.

"That's more like it. First, let's find where your house is compared to mine so we can see how far apart we are."

"About two feet," he replied, poking a teasing finger into her ribs. His reward came in the form of a cute giggle. She sure changed the shop with her presence. Imagine that.

"I'm located here, near this swamp symbol." She crimped her fingernail against the plastic, pinpointing her place. "Now where's your shop? Over here?"

Seeing she had indicated a peninsula to the south, he scooted her finger up a half-inch and tapped it a smidge further east.

"Look at that, we're a hand-width apart. Isn't that something?"

"Maybe it's God's hand-width apart, which explains how we got together in the first place. Now what about some potential locations for the corporate fishing outings? How far out should we consider?"

"Here's the map scale. Using this precise measuring device…"

"Called a pencil…" he added.

"The distance between our houses is around forty-five miles. So let's start with a fifty-mile radius. She moved her fingers out toward the eraser and rotated it around, using the bait store as the center point. "How about somewhere along the St. Lucie River inlet?"

"There's only limited public access available through there and the same across the lagoon to the east. That's high value real estate and most of the water access is private. There's the old Roosevelt Bridge fishing platform."

"That doesn't come across as very special, but at least it's restricted to pedestrian traffic. Still, there's something insincere about the roar of vehicle traffic overhead that dispels the quiet atmosphere of a fishing retreat. You're trying to make this an escape for the employees' group. I'm afraid the bridge just doesn't provide the ambiance you need."

"This makes Lake O sound better all the time. I can tell you that mileage since I drove it for the tournament. It's thirty seven miles from my house to the lake boat ramp. Maybe I should be thinking more of my potential customer base. Those folks from Palm Beach Gardens would have to travel even further."

"Well, maybe that's part of what makes it so special. You'd be introducing them to a new landscape and a lovely day of fishing." She rotated the pencil beyond the lake and pointed south.

He scratched his chin trying to think through the practicality of hauling gear all that way to fish. It sounded a little pie-in-the-sky. "I should put you in charge of public relations, Fallon, since you make it seem so doable." He nudged her shoulder with his knuckles to prompt a response, but she must have been lost in the swampland where the pencil pointed.

"I'm having a major brainstorm of an idea," she replied, blinking several times. "We have a stocked pond back behind the horse corral. Dad built an outbuilding he calls a country kitchen out beside it. The more I think about it, the more suitable it seems for something like this fishing frolic idea." She began to bounce up and down beside the counter, her eyes fixed on the map.

"What if there aren't enough fish to sustain these corporate numbers? We wouldn't want to tap out your capacity after a few runs. You might not have enough fish."

"Oh, I'll show you fish aplenty. I simply need you to come out and check, that's all. How about I invite you out for horseback riding Sunday after church?" She smiled as her figure rose and fell with the springboard action of her knees.

He grabbed her by the shoulders, but still could barely contain her enthusiasm. "I can't think of anything I'd rather do than spend Sunday with you in the swamp. Can I accept even if my horse riding might be a little on the rusty side?"

"You have to accept—or I might explode waiting to figure out this fishing frolic thing. It'll be fun. You can meet my folks, too. We'll have a cookout back on the pond and you can test the fish-ability of it all, or whatever it is you're worried about."

"If this all passes muster, I could give Motorola a call and extend them an outing as a trial offer, so they'd know they were the guinea pigs trying out something new. But make sure we get your dad on board. I get uneasy quick when the fish tank isn't mine."

"It's mine, actually. Granddaddy left it to me. I live in his log cabin back by the country kitchen. Mom and Dad live right off Loxahatchee Road on the front of the property."

"You live in a log cabin? That's downright romantic, even if it's not right on the water's edge. I guess you have your own swamp, instead. Not many enchanting girls can say that."

Her bouncing gave way to an imploring look. "I'm enchanting because I live in a cabin beside a swamp?"

That struck him as pretty irresistible. "Not the cabin or the swamp," he replied, pulling her toward him in a magnetic link-up. "It's the fish, my dear sweet Fallon. You have your own fishing pond, which is an incredible lure for any fisherman worth his salt." He could smell the rain in her hair as his lips played on her cheek. When she nuzzled into his shoulder, he explored her neck to make sure she was real. "Hey, can you read more from your Bible translation when I come out? I really liked that twenty-third Psalm you delivered over the phone. I want to hear more."

She looked up at him with clear blue eyes. "It would be my pleasure."

He considered fishing right in those blue pools. Instead, he decided to wade in and test her lips. They were perfect. The shop and its tacky details blurred under the buzz of her effect and he was taken up in it without reservation. His eyes closed as he kissed her again, the ground beneath his feet becoming more than the epicenter on their map as romance radiated from the spot. Though Fallon held her ground, the pencil gyrated and hit the floor.

Chapter 8

It could have been the way he stepped around the dirt corral, but Fallon knew her guest hadn't found his comfort level yet. Her father's gray-dappled appaloosa shifted its weight from one back foot to the other.

Court ran a hand around the back of his neck as if fighting the midday heat.

She opened the gate so they could get on the trail. Sensing adventure, her horse followed without a command, much more ready than her companion. She smoothed a hand down its neck and glanced back.

"Got any tips or suggestions to keep me from making a fool out of myself?"

"Okay. Always approach from the bow, not the stern, which is the kick zone. You're going to mount on the port side, keeping your bow lines in your hands at all times. To throttle up, touch your heels to Anvil's sides. Pull back the bow line when you want to slow or stop. Have I missed anything between start and stop?"

"What about the part where you tell me how to stay

planted in the saddle between rev up and docking for the evening?"

"That's the saddle's job, to keep you on the horse. Just hoist up there and press your knees together if it feels like you're slipping."

"I've never used my weight as an anchor before, but here goes nothing." He exhaled and toed the stirrup, then slung his right leg over the horse's spotted rump and made a perfect landing in the silver-trimmed saddle.

Fallon hadn't braced for the effect of seeing him on horseback. His build seemed perfect for it, lean and muscular. "Hold those up," she said, modeling how to hold the reins. "And we're off." She clicked a command through her teeth and both horse started out, but the appaloosa dropped a step right away. "Give your command so Anvil knows it's okay to go. You're in charge."

He gave a slight kick, sending the animal up the trail.

"Catch up and we'll ride side-by-side, so I can keep an eye on you."

"I can't say 'no' to that."

"Can you tell we're riding downhill?"

He studied the terrain. "I see a break in the pines up ahead. Something softer is clumped up after that."

"It's a cypress dome. The trees in the center grow taller because they always have water, even when the rim dries out periodically. We'll stay on the high ground and circle the dome, if it suits you."

"Except for the cleared trail, everything speaks of natural Florida the way my great-grandfather would have seen it when he came down from Georgia. I have to admit, this is starting to work its magic on me."

"You look more relaxed now. Remember, a true Florida cracker had plenty of time in the saddle."

"This cowboy stuff has its benefits—a tall perch plus a touch of swank. I could like this—if the fishing's any good."

"I sure hope fishing isn't what holds you to the landscape around here."

He smiled, until she heeled her horse and accelerated from walk to a rhythmic canter. Anvil popped into higher gear to keep pace.

Allowing him to catch up, she gave him a satisfied look and navigated the back curve of the trail.

He rode off her rear flank without further problem. "You got your wish, Calamity Jane. Nothing's holding me to the landscape but four hooves—and even they're not all touching at the same time."

"I have something else to show you." She pointed toward the upper dome and let the tangle of branches speak to its own grandeur.

"Eagle nest? Or maybe osprey, the fish hawk," he guessed. While they were watching, a white-headed bird flew onto the nest and disappeared over the rim.

"Not big enough for an eagle," she replied. "That means you're not the first fisherman to stake a claim out here today."

"Maybe I'll show him a thing or two down by the pond."

"Maybe so." She guided her horse up the trail and soon found him tucked up right beside her, humming under his breath. There was no way to miss his cozy companionship now, as it spread all over the trail. The corral came back into sight much too soon.

~

"This is the Taj Mahal of log cabins, if there ever was one." Court's gaze picked out one attractive feature after another. A braid of wood arched over the cook stove and the refrigerator disappeared into matching cabinetry. An antler chandelier hung above an irregular slab of cypress wood posing as the dining room table. Climbing from the open kitchen and living area, a heavy-beamed stairway rose to a loft. "Is your room up there?"

"My bedroom and my office, which could be a nursery, should I ever decide to nest." Her fingers crooked the air, adding quote marks to her last word.

He took a long drink of lemonade and thought it over. "Well, in that case, you're all set. All you need is Daniel Boone to break the plane of your front door and your swamp family can commence."

"Guess I'll be the judge of that." She blushed and led him to the picture window. "Here's the Taj Mahal's reflecting pool. Somehow, it's not as haughty or contrived."

"Still, it's every bit as effective as a sky-mirror. The view's sensational."

"I see all kinds of wildlife back here like bobcat, deer, and otter, plus the resident brigade of pond turtles. I feed the birds off the corner of the porch during migration. It gives me a little company before I pull out in the morning for my commute."

"Do you spend much time with your parents?"

"Mainly weekends. Sometimes, Mom and I go shopping together on Tuesdays. It's a bit of a drive over to the nearest store, so we share the expense and have some girl time."

"I suppose I'm carving into some of that weekend

time block. Have they noticed?" This could be a walk through a spilt box of hooks, especially if he treaded on father-daughter territory.

She opened the side door and walked out to a small concrete patio. "Oh, they've noticed, and they're happy about it. I thought this would make a great place for pole racks or gear storage. We can move it inside at the end of the day or lock it away in the back closet there."

"What about that place?" He pointed to a large shed with an overhanging porch. "It could have some potential."

"That's where we're going to cook for the people, silly. That's the country kitchen, half-outdoor and half-indoor—to beat the elements either way, as my granddaddy used to say."

"Smart man," he replied, making wide strides to go check out the building. The door gave a creak and relented to his shoulder, opening to a vast space with a row of stainless steel kitchen appliances hunkered at the far end.

"We could seat fifty-five to sixty people easily. The rest would have to sit on the front porch or outside at the picnic tables. Imagine having a rollicking game of Butterfly Bingo in here after the fishing contest. The possibilities are endless."

He came to stand by her, studying the layout as his mind raced. To hedge his enthusiasm, he placed a hand on her back and tried to anchor himself mentally. A panoramic band of horizontal glass broke the walls on both sides of the front door. He eyed the grounds all the way down to the pond. "Where would those picnic tables be?"

She plucked his bicep with her middle finger. "Those

have yet to be built by the frolic leader, but he's working up a plan even as we speak." She smiled and put her glass down on a rustic end table to free her hands.

When the double doors swung open at her touch, the effect moved him. There sat the pond, front and center, inviting the occupants to come visit. How stunning.

"I think it's time for your ultimate test, don't you?"

"Fish don't fail me now." He'd never been as eager to drop a line as he was right then. A surge of purpose and a dusting of fate swirled together in summer's heat to fire his imagination. That this location came wrapped with Fallon's involvement fell more than a perk, as she fanned his dream-fire with a well-aimed breeze. Running before he knew it, he imagined the pole in his hands. This had the makings of a major strike, and he aimed to give it his full professional evaluation.

Court reached over the side of the truck and retrieved two poles, one more than necessary, but Fallon might want to join in the fun. He caught the tackle box's handle and away he ran to size up the fishing hole. Aiming straight across, he motioned her over. He touched a finger to his lips for quiet and gave her the smaller pole. Throwing his tackle box open, he reviewed the selection.

Before he could switch out his hook for an artificial lure, she had her line cocked back to cast. "What's your bait?"

She nodded to the ground beside him where a plastic bag full of a sliced hot dog rested. "That's never going to cut it. Try something smarter."

She let loose the rig and it sailed off about fifteen feet, dimpling the water as it landed. In three seconds, the bobber disappeared and Fallon laughed as she set the hook to start reeling. "Come on in, the water's fine! Go ahead and use the hot dog. These fish are hungry." When her reeling proved inadequate, she backed up along the shore. Finally, a sizeable bluegill emerged hooked through its top lip.

He clapped twice and loaded his rig with pauper bait, sending it sailing as he knelt to release her catch.

"No, I'll do it. Go fight your own battles."

His strike took seven seconds and the bobber took an angry yank. With the fish putting up a fuss, he settled into flattened terrain on the bank. He wasn't disappointed in the least when a decent long-eared sunfish made an appearance at the water's edge.

"Now it's one to one. Are you going to fish or cut bait, mister?"

He looked up to catch her provocative challenge. Something shifted beyond sporting pleasure inside. "The bait's already cut, chatterbox. Bring your best game next to mine."

"First one to ten wins. Better be quick about it, Bait Crate." She reached for another pinch of meat as the bluegill flopped back into the water.

He tossed the sunfish further than necessary in his exuberance to match her challenge. Pinching the hot dog slice into thirds, he laced a tiny portion onto the silver barb and swung it toward the pond. Fisherman's fate now on his side, he had his next success while her bobber sat lifeless. "That's two for me."

He landed the fish. Loving the hastened rhythm, he peeled a small bass off and loaded a bigger chunk of meat. He took three strides across the bank and let it rip through the air. The strike came on contact. *This place is incredible.* Seven fish later, he clapped his hands as blood pulsed through his body on heightened alert.

Fallon released her latest catch—number nine—and swished her hands through the water to wash off the slime. When she stood, he tipped her toward the water, his hands locking on her hips with a rescuer's grip. She gasped and tried to shift back toward land off-balance.

He held her at angles to the splash zone. "Winner calls the prize."

"Not a dousing." She clamped her hands over his wrists.

One look over her shoulder settled it for him. "I've got this," he replied, ready to celebrate. His nose trekked over a field of freckles until his lips landed to exact their prize directly on hers. His hands yielded only enough maneuver space for her to shift around to face him. When she began to kiss him back with a starvation akin to how the fish had hit, the parallel wasn't lost on him. He'd found fishing nirvana at long last, a remarkable sensation.

Chapter 9

Fallon shot a worried glance at Court as several papers moved between the two men. She busied her pencil with random swirls.

"Don't sell your services too cheap," Warren said.

"Wow, Dad. You've really done your homework. "The equipment rental business must have been slow midweek." Fallon couldn't get a read on Court as he skipped from page to page. Her pencil began to etch the name "Bait Crate" across the paper's header.

Her mother flipped a page on her notepad and jotted something down. "I think corporate outings might be a lucrative aside for the bait shop."

"Janine's right, Court. These corporate folks are always looking for the next experience, so why not take them back to the land—or water in this case. Indoor parties are boring and overdone. And the beach? Well, the whole state's a beach. Everybody's done that."

"As much as I love Lake O, to get the entire employees' club out on the water would take an armada, even on pontoon boats," Court said. "Once the pieces started falling into place, I could see the flaws with that destination. But here we'd have parking, cooking, fishing, and game-playing all taken care of, literally with the spread you already have."

"Not to mention horseback riding made possible with a loan from across the road," Fallon added. "I'd like to keep that option open and get it into the brochure."

"Leave Doug Nelson to me," Janine insisted, making a note of it. "He's eaten a jar of my orange marmalade every Christmas for the past twenty-five years. That should be good for some type of payback. His horses probably need the exercise."

Court pulled closer to the table. "Fallon, could you design the brochure?"

"You bet. If it rains this coming week, I can knock it out at work. Otherwise, I'll do it for homework and e-mail it to dad's office."

"I'll be glad to print the draft," Warren replied, "but once you get it like you want it, let's go with something slicker than what I can produce in-house. There's a small printer near us. Easy folks to work with and they're inexpensive."

"Have you thought about what to name this?" Janine asked.

Fallon smiled and displayed the paper she'd been doodling on.

"Bait Crate Fishing Frolics," Court said. "I like it—simple and self-explanatory."

"Plus slightly old-fashioned," Fallon added. "We could add some old-timey props for a photo station and work it into the games, too. You know—tug-of-war, horseshoes or badminton." Her enthusiasm must have been showing, because Court flashed a wink her way.

"I can't believe you mentioned horseshoes, Fallon. Your grandpa always wanted to have a set of pits out by the kitchen building," her father admitted. "I'll make sure that happens. Plus we can add newer games, like that ladderball toss. It's easy and only has a few moving parts to keep up with. People enjoy throwing games."

"What about parking?" Court asked. He leaned over the aerial and almost bumped heads with Warren as they examined the layout.

Fallon reached past him to run her pencil eraser up and down the main driveway. "No need to take up unnecessary real estate for cars."

"Pulling in spaces off the main drive is perfect," Warren replied, "because there's plenty of gravel there already. Use the lawn for games. This is really coming together. You two work out the rest of the details and get back to us on our part." He snapped his fingers and landed his elbow on the tabletop, his arm upright.

When Court pulled back with a questioning look, Fallon laughed. "He's challenging you. Dad wants to arm wrestle to seal the deal."

"Oh, Warren." Janine stood. "I'll bring in dessert now."

"It's not a problem, ma'am," Court replied. He pressed his tanned arm into position and regarded his opponent.

Fallon rolled her eyes, but any objection would have been futile. She recognized that her dad had her best interest in mind, even if he had a peculiar way of showing it.

"Say when, Fallon, if your friend's ready," Warren said in a slow, dry drawl. He crinkled his cheek for effect.

Court chewed the tip of a toothpick, poker-faced.

It struck her that these two combatants deserved each other. Exhaling, she scraped her chair closer and placed her arm on the table like a referee. "On your mark, get set, go!" She slapped the tabletop. Her father's forearm creased when his muscles tightened under his sleeve while Court's arm flexed like steel. The clamped hands drifted off first one side and then the other. Her dad's neck reddened as he held his breath for rigid strength. Court didn't flinch, channeling his effort. After fifteen seconds, crinkles deepened at the corners of his eyes. Her father's neck veins bulged. Almost a minute went by and the battle raged on.

"Who wants homemade mango ice cream?" Janine asked, stepping back into the dining room. Fallon lifted a finger to be counted in and the motion somehow broke the stalemate.

Court flattened her father's hand onto the tabletop with a loud pop of his knuckles, falling exhausted across her refereeing arm. She laughed and patted his shoulder to dub him the winner.

"Must have ice cream," Court said, his lips moving against her arm. The rest of his body sat like a lump off the end of the table.

"Loser gets served first," Warren replied short of breath. Everyone laughed as balled scoops of orange-colored sherbet danced around delicate footed glass bowls delivered by the hand of the hostess. "What a way to take my lumps."

After Fallon passed Court a dish of mounded dessert, she placed hers against Warren's overheated neck.

"Thank you, baby. I'll try to redeem my honor

another day.”

“This Loxahatchee tribe is a hard one to break into.” Court took a nip at the creamy treat. “Ummm. But so worth it.” His gaze darted toward her for a split second, and then fell back onto his desert bowl.

Turning her spoon upside down, she emptied the sweet concoction onto her tongue while her mind raced ahead to her last surprise of the day. A coastal boy away from his water zone, he seemed pretty happy being landlocked today, and she planned to keep it that way.

~

Court hesitated by her front door in the duskiness of nightfall. “You didn’t forget my request for the reading, did you?”

“It’s not time to close the gate yet,” Fallon replied with a smile. “Come in and take a seat. I’ll get my Bible.” She tucked the notepad into the crook of her arm and skittered up the sturdy stairs. She tossed him a wave from the top landing and disappeared from view. Words of a slow-tempo praise song soon drifted down.

He examined the seating options and selected a leather chaise that undulated like the ocean. Almost too modern for the cabin, it held enough width for them to fit side by side. Eyeing the cavernous room, he settled in for his requested treat. When her socked feet padded back down, he tapped the open side of the chaise for her to join him.

“Try this for maximum comfort,” she suggested, offering a small pillow that had “God Be Near” stitched across its middle.

He raised his head and she placed it under the crook of his neck. The fit proved kingly and he moaned.

"I brought my pillow to remind us that this was a spiritual endeavor, this sharing of divine words."

"Soothe the beast within me by bringing thy fair reading, my loft angel. On my honor, I shall endeavor to resist any fleshly urges. He that has ears, let him hear—as Jesus said."

"Okay, I guess it's safe for me to perch beside you." She slid onto the chaise. Her knees held the Bible up and she opened the book midway.

Comforted by her contact, he closed his eyes and drifted upward in attitude.

"A song of God's deliverance for boaters," she began, "from Psalm one hundred-seven. A select brotherhood of the redeemed ply the open waters with their boats, making their livelihood upon the vast seas. That is where God is most evident to them, on the shimmering sensation of his water-columned wonder. He speaks and his breath ripples the waves toward shore. Should his voice deepen against the elements, a tempest breaks forth."

Tranquil calm slipped to something deeper. Court placed his hand over hers on the Bible, connecting them under the Word of God. With his mind attuned to her every utterance, visions of glistening waters became hooded by graying skies that skittered through his mind's eye.

She hesitated only a heartbeat's duration. "Forced to ride the storm out crest-to-trough and back again, their hearts tremble like a killdeer's wing-flutter. The pitching boat ensnares their equilibrium and casts their confidence overboard, leaden with worry. Shipwrecked on the reef of despair, they call out for the Lord's mercy, and he hears them to end the calamity."

As if to claim the mercy her words offered, he curled his fingers into hers.

She gave them a faint squeeze and took a breath. "He tamps the bucking waves down with his hand and commands the wind to whisper. Taking heart that the storm has ended, the boatmen allow God to lead them to safe haven."

With safety's arrival, Court lifted her hand and touched a gentle kiss to her knuckles, like a sailor would kiss dry land after such an ordeal.

Her breathing became shallow and she cleared her throat to continue. "Let your thanksgiving flow along an endless canal for the love he extends to the brotherhood of boaters. His love is aimed for *you* and his deeds promise to be more generous than the lake's depths. May your praise splash the surface of his mighty waters and may God be lifted up when the lock gates open to you. Be among the wise that understand the cycle from crest to Creator—and ever hold his love high." Silence stepped in as she closed the book and let it rest against her ribs, lowering her legs to stretch beside him.

In unhurried reflection, Court allowed the words to drift through him. They all seemed written for him, like God spoke to him through Fallon's interpretation. The effect proved both contemplative and satisfying. Even more wondrous, she seemed devoted to him, inside-out from the soul. The awareness could not be trivialized by outward touch, but when she sniffed, he yearned to wrap her in his arms.

"May I hold you?" he asked, barely a whisper. He released his finger grip and slid one arm under her shoulders. She turned and snuggled to his side, the

Bible wedged between them like an everlasting presence. His other arm clasped around her to close the circle. There he remained for a glorious stretch of time, adrift on God's generosity. With the night smelling of fresh rain, one tempest had passed, the personal storm called loneliness.

Chapter 10

Tuesday came with the dusky odor of marine-based paint. Fallon stretched over the concrete flank of the canal lock balancing a brush in her hand. The causeway between locks had only a visitor or two as the midmorning sun built a solid case for more shady surroundings. Reaching for the next number on the water level calibration, her brush fell a few inches short.

"Come to me, fifteen feet. You need repainting and I need to get done." She shifted on the concrete apron and managed a few more inches to her reach. A touch of the black-tipped brush proved she had succeeded in moving one more foot down the gauge. With a steady push, she filled the tens unit and pulled back up to wet the brush with more paint. Action in the upper canal snagged her attention where the Fish and Game boat was working the last vessels released from the lock. Permit checks looked like busy work from there.

"Uh-oh, an annoying fly and I've got wet paint showing. Maybe he won't pester me up here," she muttered. The five digit proved troublesome, having both straight lines and curves. She held her edge and kept the contact even bottom-upwards as she crowned the number with its flattop. "I'll never make fourteen at this rate."

She stood to assess boat traffic on the lower canal where a small motorboat operator tethered his lines with Charlie's help. Two more boats were idling into the lock zone, giving her ten minutes to get this done. Determined to get fourteen under her belt, she dropped and stretched like a superhero, teetering on the edge to get positioned. With a flick of her wrist, the one received paint. Now if she could get the four in the black paint zone.

"Morning Ms. McKenzie. Nice day for a paint party," a man said below.

She glanced over to find Kit Rawlings ogling up at her, so she flattened her gaping shirt with the butt of her right hand. Taking the brush with her left hand, she striped the cross bar of the number four and gave it a stem to stand on, which was more than she had.

"I can appreciate that you're in a compromised position, Fallon. Could I offer the services of my boat to provide access to the lower scale? Charlie's only got one boat left. Then he'll need to flood the lock."

She stood to assess the situation through her own rubric. Charlie hadn't gotten the third boat's lines in hand yet, so she still had most of her ten minutes. Trouble was, she couldn't reach any more of the gauge calibrations. It would take her half an hour to go get the Corps work barge in place to finish.

"You know my boat can't stay here once the lock is flooding. Right?"

"That's right, Mr. Rawlings. Our rule, not yours, but thanks for remembering."

"So come on. What'd you say to a little team effort twixt your agency and mine?" He smiled and motioned for the paint can, almost reaching up to number twelve. Gritting her teeth, she scooped up the pail and lowered it. She stuck the brush in a plastic baggie and secured it in her shirt pocket, then climbed down the rungs for Corps use only. She'd have to come back another time and repaint the word "Restricted."

The boat shifted back to receive her, so Fallon stepped on deck, refusing his offered hand. She spied the paint can and grabbed it as she made her way to the bow. "I'll work from up here."

"Fine. That view should be ideal for me."

She looked away, but not before she saw a smile crook into his cheek like some redneck voyeur. Her regret deepened for having taken the quick way out.

"You need me to hold anything?"

"No, I've got it. You tend the boat and keep me as close as you can."

"Gladly. Sure never thought you'd say something so cuddly, but I'm a patient man."

"I meant close to the wall where I'm painting. Nothing more." With her teeth clenched to avoid further banter, she dipped the brush and made quick work of ten, eleven, and twelve. When she reached for thirteen, even standing on the gunwale rail left it out of reach.

"You need either a boost or a stool now." He moved away from the helm. "All I've got is this gas can and it's too rounded on top. Let me give you a boost. You're a fast painter."

"No way."

"Well, what's your idea, Miss Painted-into-a-Corner?" He threw his hands up in surrender and held them there awaiting an answer.

She glanced between the railing and the unlucky number. She needed a foot of height. "Come over here on this side and kneel down. I'll stand on your leg and paint as fast as I can. Will you do it?"

"If you take your shoes off, I'll be happy to." He readily took a kneeling position.

She'd obligated herself too deeply to back out now, so she jacked off her work boots, dipped the brush, and stepped up. In seconds, the one was completed and she dropped back onto the deck. As she bent to reload the brush, she caught him reaching for her.

"Don't—or you'll be sorry. Keep it professional." Her tone sharp, she made direct eye contact so he'd know better than cross her up. Moving toward the concrete wall, she stepped up unaided and got the top loop of the three painted before his hand trespassed on the back of her right thigh.

"You're shaking. Let me keep you steady so you can finish." He patted her leg. "You're sure tone. Baby, I like that."

The bottom curl on the three couldn't fill in fast enough as her hand wanted to toss the brush and form a fist to quell his freshness. Before she could step down, he had both hands around her calves massaging them at his pleasure. "Take me to the dock or I'm writing up a complaint for inappropriate behavior," she said, striding toward the stern as far away from him as she could get.

Charlie sounded the ready bell, so the fisheries warden found his place behind the console to depart.

Having opted for the shortcut instead of being self-reliant, she accepted the blame. She'd given him an inch and he took a thigh. *Shame on me.*

By the time they'd made the dock, fury shook her north to south. The heat of the day escalated that reactive steam by a factor of ten. Plus, she had black paint all over her uniform. Since she needed her boots, she'd have to brave her way past him to make the retrieval. She waited until the dock lay within reach. "Let me get my boots and I'll be out of your way." She brushed past him, found the boots, and stomped them on with a single shove of each foot.

"The job between you and me ain't finished, Fallon. You just need to warm up to the fact that it's gonna happen someday." He started to say more, but a sharp motion on the dock severed the words.

Court pulled her out of the boat and into his arms. "You're done, Rawlings. Go make yourself scarce." His foot shoved the gunwale and the boat rocked away from the pilings.

"This is my lake, bait boy. Maybe *you'd* better skedaddle and leave the fish—and the women—to a better man."

Conscious of being in uniform, Fallon jerked from Court's grip and stepped toward the ramp where Liam waited for his bait shipment. The sound of a boat ramping out to open water brought relief. Her shoulders shook involuntarily.

"Low life." Liam shifted his hat on his head. "Charlie and I watched the whole thing from the tower. He said you should file a report to put that creep's supervisor on alert." The teen shook his head.

Court clamped a hand on his shoulder. "Do what

your heart tells you, Fallon. We can talk it out when I get back this afternoon, if it helps." He searched her face but didn't try to touch her. After motioning to her cheek, he drew a finger down his nose.

"I'll go get cleaned up. Maybe Sheri can help me."

"She's in the back office," Liam replied. "You look like a fighter with face paint on."

"For a hot second there, I thought about it. Not too Christian of me, right?"

"No, but it held a pretty high entertainment factor, because when I walked up, all bets were on you," Court admitted.

His sheepish grin did nothing to restore her faith in mankind. Okay, almost nothing. When he gestured for her to take the lead up the ramp, she couldn't get there fast enough. Backstage was her forte. She'd never wanted to shine from center stage or front deck.

~

The screen door to the bait shop flew open and Court spotted the tousled mop-head who lived next door as she made her daily appearance.

"Hey. What's shaking down here besides wigglers, I mean?" She stopped long enough to finger some of the squiggly plastic lures for their gooey texture.

"Hi Audie. Some last-minute fishermen left out before the tide drops too far. Are you up to anything good?" He handed her a box a bobbers and nodded toward a side shelf.

The girl busied her hands with the playful assignment, touching the crooked bobbers to shift their red-meets-white horizons to align. "Naw, mom says I'm not being good today. I had a little incident with my sister at lunch and now I have to go spend the rest of this week with Aunt Kiera down in Jupiter."

"She's getting rid of you to her druggie sister? Like that's some promising solution." He slammed down a can and it made more noise than he'd intended.

"I think she's dried out now. Anyway, I get to go to the beach all I want, so it's cool with me." She held her hands up over the bobber box like she was casting a spell over it. "Anything else for me to do?"

"Would you feed the fish in the front pond? I'm almost done here and we can do the back pond together. Okay?" He looked up from the register long enough to catch her reaction. He wouldn't force her to do chores, after all. She volunteered and could be pretty good help if she set her mind to it.

"For you, Court-meister, I willingly slave away. Did you see Fallon on your bait run with Liam today?" Her eyebrows took turns arching to punctuate her question.

"I did. She had a little paint job go bad when she tried to use a human ladder that proved to be all hands and no manners."

"Better to do the work yourself, then nobody hassles you."

"You have a point there, kiddo. But remember, I want you to use the buddy system when you go to the beach. That's a lot of responsibility for a twelve-year old. Here's the key to the feed box. Just leave it in the lock and I'll retrieve it when I come out. Now scoot and let me count out the drawer."

"I'm going already," she replied, giving him a brooding look. She took the key and stomped through the back room. "Hey, should I give this thieving pelican the treatment?"

"Whoop it up, girl. He's eating our profits back

there." He pulled out the ones, and then a thinner stack of fives. The girl screamed like a banshee and clanged the trashcan lids together just like he'd taught her. Having lost count, he started again and recorded it before her next interruption.

"Did Carter's baby come today?"

"No baby yet. Due date's tomorrow, so it could be soon." The tens came out next, all four of them. Too thin to call a stack, he recorded the subtotal. There were no twenties. They needed a fishing tournament to increase sales. That wouldn't happen until the Fourth of July tournament, three long weeks away. Maybe he'd better accelerate his fishing frolic plans.

His gaze settled on the clock above the entrance. He had half an hour to make that call to Motorola, thinking he could talk it up without a brochure in hand. Since this would be his first event, he could tailor it to their expectations and back costs into the selected options. Unsure about the horses, he walked to the back door to find Audie. She lay out on the plank dock, rolling fish food pellets into the water below. The water's surface simply bubbled with gulping fish lips.

"Be out in a few minutes, Audie. I've got to make a phone call before the workday ends."

"Okay, Court. I'll keep these guys entertained until you get out here." She flipped her wrist and a few more pellets spun into the water.

He brought up the number and sent the call. "Mr. Shaw? This is Court Reynolds from the Bait Crate. If you have a few minutes, I'd like to discuss the possibility of a fishing outing for your employee club, if you're still interested." His ears strained to hear the response and when it came in the affirmative, his blood pressure shot up a few points.

"I think I found just the place in Loxahatchee, secluded and loaded with fish. But you guys would be our guinea pigs as we test out the location. Let me give you the entertainment venues, and then we'll talk about food options." He wiped his upper lip as he gauged the interest level coming back to him. "Yes, sir, we'll have fish aplenty, to catch and to eat. It doesn't get any fresher than that, does it?"

He pulled out the notepad to go over the specifics and the doodle Fallon had sketched across the header caught his eye. Part of him went liquid. His dream came to the forefront as he went down the checklist she had produced, getting input on each item. Anytime the executive made a suggestion, he added it to their list. Satisfaction started to build, and by the end of the phone call, his feet barely touched the ground. Leaping from the back stoop, his celebratory whoop practically scared Audie off the dock.

"Jiminy Cricket! What's got after you?"

"Excited about the new area Bait Crate is branching off into—corporate fishing parties."

"People pay to go fish at a party?"

"Well, we'll have games and horseback riding, and then we'll feed them after they've fished. It might be a lot of work to get set up, but I'm excited to see what kind of business we can drum up. Fallon has a great pond at her ranch, so we're starting there with the first party." He walked her over to the back pond and took some of the pellets.

The girl's bottom lip poked out. "I see the truth behind it. She's stealing you from us." She slung a handful of food across the pond and the fish scattered to retrieve it.

"Hey, nobody's stealing anything. We have to grow the business or Carter's new baby won't have enough food to eat. Does that sound reasonable?'

"Babies don't eat real food for a long, long time. I know you're going to be spending less time around here. Just admit it." Her pout set deeper as she flung more pellets.

"I'll be here solid for the next two weeks because Carter can't. If you had behaved, you'd be around too so we could work together. As it is, you're on the naughty mat at your aunt's house for the rest of this week."

"By naughty mat you mean beach towel. I'm heading for the beach and nothing's going to stop me." She emptied her container of pellets all in one place and caused the baitfish to pile up on each other's backs.

"Where's your good sense?" he asked, perturbed. A grown man should be better at rendering logic than a twelve-year old. He tried to rally his position. "Buddy system around water—always. It doesn't matter if it's a pond or the big blue ocean. At least assure me that I've managed to get that much through this thick head of yours." He rapped his knuckles across her tangled hair.

She caught his fist with both hands. "I'll be back to help you. You're lost without me."

"Talk about tough," he replied, wedging her head into a wrestler's hold until she laughed. All skin, bones, and attitude, he knew she was a good kid, but wondered if anyone else noticed.

~

"Sorry to be a self-promoter, but I'm calling to invite you out Saturday afternoon for my birthday barbeque,"

Fallon said, her tone teasing. "It's really a ploy. Dad wants you here to help him weld together a couple of fishing pole racks. He found some schematic in a magazine and wants to make it happen. I think he's found his new best friend, somebody to play with down by the pond."

"That sounds fantastic, even if I have to close up the shop early to get out there. Tessa will be overdue by then, so Carter's liable to be scarce. I'll talk to Dad and see if he'll pull a shift to free me up. If he finds out I'm welding fishing racks, he might want to come with me. He's a project nut."

"We'll have to get them together—maybe when we launch the fishing frolic. Any word back from Motorola?" Her stomach tensed, so she leaned back in the kitchen chair. The odor of discarded onions bothered her, so she tied the trash liner and stood to take it out.

"Oh yeah, we have a date for the kickoff event on June twenty-eighth. It seems crazy to give us less than three weeks to pull this together, but Mr. Shaw had already announced the date to the employees' club, so off we plunge into experimental launch."

"Okay, now I'm a little nervous about my food quantities. We might have to spend some time Saturday night after dinner going through my list. Do you mind mixing business with pleasure?" She opened the back door and tossed out the trash.

"Not if both are with you. I take it men are back in your good graces."

"Select men are. Others might be on report to my immediate supervisor as a precautionary measure. I'm putting that incident behind me. Otherwise I'd simmer over it and ruin what's being blessed in my life right now. I hope I didn't send any scathing glances in your direction down on the dock, but thank you for stepping in when you did."

"I saw the tempest in your eyes, so I steered clear. It was all I could do not to board Rawlings' boat and give him the knuckle punch he deserved."

"Well, that would have been a protocol breach not in our favor. Charlie thought I handled the whole thing like a professional, plus he signed my in-house report. Case closed."

"Great, next topic then. What would you like for your birthday? A puppy?"

"Court, don't you dare. I'm gone all day at the locks. How fair would that be to a puppy? How about something pretty?"

"Guys don't have a 'pretty' detection gene, but I'm up for the challenge. What time did you want me out? How about after three? The shop gets slow around then."

"That's great. I'll tell dad to expect you shy of four o'clock, so you don't have to rip the pavement up on I-95. Oh, he said to bring work gloves." Fallon slipped back into the kitchen chair and retrieved a blank pad to sketch down a few ideas. Her doodling started up and she twirled the letters together that spelled out the event name.

"Work gloves, a pretty present, and possibly a birthday balloon." He paused to chuckle.

His tone melted her a bit and she didn't want the conversation to end. "Could I trade the balloon in for a few more minutes on the phone?" Somehow the longing in her heart seeped into her voice without permission, but it was too late to take back the request. She laid the phone on her cheek.

He made a throaty adjustment. "Go over to that chaise thing where we sat the other night. I want to tell you what Lake O looked like today on our bait run. Close your eyes so you can see it with me."

"Hold on a second," she replied, hastening over to the chaise. The little "God Be Near" pillow sat right in the middle, so she hugged it to her chest. "All set. Take me with you." It seemed a small request of companionable proportion, a heart merger with a special friend. In no time, she found herself afloat with his detailed rendering, his voice a buoy on the surface.

Chapter 11

Court turned down the drive toward the birthday party, checking the gravel treatment on each side of the drive as he approached the log cabin. When he pulled closer, he saw a white canopy framing the sky by the outdoor kitchen. Warren backed out of the front door dragging an orange power cord toward a work area under the lean-to roof. A welding machine stood nearby. Fallon appeared toting one corner of a craft table while Janine trailed. He parked and jogged to the action in time to help set the table under the canopy. "Are we going fancy for the party?"

"More like practicing for the fishing frolic," Janine replied.

Fallon stepped to his side of the table and gave him a delightful hug. She wore a scent that made him think of cake batter, maybe vanilla. When he took a second sniff, she laughed and swatted him back.

"Let's get the chairs, sweetie," Janine said.

"That's me—not you," Fallon replied, tugging his arm. "Your job is right over there with Dad. Try to keep up, will you?" She laughed and it sounded like music.

He caught her nose between two knuckles and gave it a tug, noticing how her eyes simply twinkled today. His gaze dropped down the length of her smooth neck and he enjoyed the tiny teardrop pearl dangling from her choker necklace. A hollow cove sat at the base of her throat, reminding him of the curve of a spoon lure. He had the urge to run his thumb through it to see what would happen. For now, he'd leave it to the pearl, but he might have to go exploring later. "Let me get my gloves. Should I get the puppy out now or leave it in the truck?"

"No puppy," Fallon replied, her tone firm.

He laughed and slapped his hands together as she waggled a finger at him and disappeared back into the log cabin. He returned to the kitchen porch with his gloves and a fishing pole for sizing purposes.

"Oh, thanks for bringing the pole out," Warren said. "I hadn't thought to question the schematic." He leaned a flat metal panel against the saw horse. He nodded and Court helped lift the first piece in place. "Let me show you the plans so you can get a feel for what we're doing here. Know how to use this thing?" He nodded toward the welding torch.

Uncertainty flipped under his ribcage, but Court knew to be honest. "No, sir. Not at all. My grandfather worked on boat hulls in the local shipyard, but his specialty was wood, not metalwork. I did plenty of sanding under his direction, but no welding."

"Perfect then. It'll be my treat to teach you, and I'll enjoy every minute of it, too. We've had a lot of girl goings-on out here and not enough man stuff. You're evening out the odds for me, and I plan to savor that turn of the tide."

"Glad to take your instruction. These rod racks are a top-notch idea, sir. Thank you for thinking ahead."

"You'll find me to be very systematic. Nothing grates my craw worse than somebody trying to fly by the seat of their pants. You can't run a business like that, a successful one anyway. I hope you can see the wisdom in my approach." Warren handed him the schematic and pulled the welding tank closer.

Donning a heavy yellow shirt, he slid the welding helmet in place and lowered a shield. "Our first seam is right here, front panel to side panel. I'll lay down this bead and you watch from a couple steps back. Got any sunglasses in the truck? You're not supposed to look directly at the torch flame."

Court jogged back to the truck to retrieve his sunglasses. The cab had heated up in the afternoon sun, so he decided to deliver the flower bouquet to the table crew. Fallon returned to the yard with a chair in each arm, heading for the canopy as Janine snapped a red cloth across the craft table.

"Here's to being a reflection of true beauty," he said, whirling the bouquet from around his back. A miniature purple iris nearly touched her chin and made her eyes seem bluer by comparison. Warren made an impatient sound from under the porch, so he kissed her forehead and reported back to duty. He overheard Janine's favorable remark just before Warren lit the torch and gave him a new arena of play. Fire may have been fascinating before, but what it did to metal at flame tip proved downright mesmerizing. Half an hour later, the rack had everything but handles and a bottom.

"Warren, the grill's ready," Janine said in passing.

"I'll get the vegetables cut. The meat is ready. Come with me and give the kids some time together."

Court shucked his gloves and eyed the masterpiece as Warren followed his wife inside.

"How's it coming over here?" Fallon stepped under the porch's overhang. "Wow. It looks great. That will pay dividends when we're in a hurry and can pull the rack out of storage all ready to go."

"I'm over-the-top about all of it, and this is certainly the latest masterpiece. I can't believe we're going to take a stab at this in a few short weeks, something I've been thinking about for years. Speaking of years, how many is my birthday girl celebrating today, if I can ask without any backlash?" He tossed his gloves on the welder to free his hands.

"Twenty-eight, so I'm lagging still behind you a couple of years. Does that seem about right?" Her eyes sparkled with interest, making her hard to resist.

Warren banged back out the kitchen door with a platter of steaks. "Hope a fisherman doesn't have anything against beef."

"Are you kidding?"

"Nothing smells better cooking on a grill, in my opinion." As if to validate his comment, Warren waved the grilling tool like a king's scepter and stalked off to start the aroma wafting.

"Help me! I've got a situation here," Janine said, leaning out the door. The white tea towel wrapped her left hand had blood leaking through. "I cut my thumb trying to get the vegetables chopped for the skewers. Somebody's going to have to take my place while I go get this cleaned up. Fallon honey, can I use your bathroom?"

Court froze at the sight of bright red blood, even though it wasn't dripping.

Yes, Mom. Court and I will get the kabobs ready, unless you need me."

"No, I'll handle it. Try to get those veggies to your father by the time he's ready to turn the steaks, if you can. Where are your bandages?"

"Second drawer on the left. Don't worry about us. We work fairly well together. I'll tell Dad what's going on, so he won't fuss." Fallon headed for the grill while Janine trotted toward the cabin, leaving him alone on the porch. He entered the kitchen intent on washing his hands and stepped up to a blood bath left in the sink. A shot from the sprayer nozzle washed everything away but the nausea. He hunted under the cabinet for something to disinfect the surfaces. Recognizing the cleaner, he chose a blue spray bottle and had the job done by the time Fallon appeared.

She picked up on his punk expression. "Hope it wasn't too messy."

"Sorry. I don't do blood well. Give me fish guts any day of the week."

"Blood sends a different message to the brain. Now that you've survived all those sharp edges while welding, do you think you can trust a simple kitchen knife?"

"Not that one," he replied, pointing to the culprit of Janine's calamity. "Have anything on the dull side?" He managed to hook a half-smile and she laughed, producing another utensil from the top drawer. It looked like it hadn't been sharpened since the big war. "Now I'm in business. Give me the zucchini. You take the menacing mushrooms."

"I've got to pull you out of this phobic funk. How about I thank you for my flowers?"

He cut the end off a zucchini. "Well, I kind of have my hands full here." The zucchini succumbed in thick slices.

"Fortunately for you, hands aren't necessary." She leaned in and placed a quick peck on his cheek, but the sparkle in her eye didn't seem satisfied afterward.

"I'll have to charge one of those per flower, unless you want to up your payment plan."

"Want to and plan to," she replied. A mushroom split in half and rolled away in freedom. She flattened the knife against the cutting board and left it.

As she moved face-to-face, he took a break. OSHA would have been proud of him, as he released the knife so he wouldn't be driving it under the influence of her next kiss. It lasted long enough to make the full payment.

"Too bad daddy needs the veggies soon or I could really get sidetracked with such a handsome work associate."

"Maybe twenty-eight is the year of your sidetrack," he teased, reclaiming his knife. "I'm switching to peppers next, if you'll do the onions. Then we can start loading the skewers."

"Goodness me, you're as bad as daddy is with all the systematic approach."

"You're the one working for the regulatory agency, not me. I'm a simple fisherman." He bit his bottom lip to stifle a smile.

She winged him with her elbow and beheaded several more lowly mushrooms. "The flowers were sweet of you." She rinsed the red and green peppers and sat them in front of him.

They reminded him of stop and go signs, and left him to figure out which one was blinking his way. A third choice—caution—came to mind. "Spending time with you on your special day is my real motivation. I don't think we need flowers or steaks to make that stand out. But you deserve the special treatment, which is something I plan to whisper in your ear later."

He allowed all toying pretense to drain from his expression as she gazed up into his eyes. The exchange pumped some adrenalin into his veins and he tore into the peppers without mercy. When a tear slipped down her cheek while cutting the onions, he didn't question the reason why.

Soon smoke from the grill left a curtain between the cave-dwelling hunter-gatherers and the more delicate womenfolk under the canopy. Warren placed him in charge of the skewers. If it hadn't been for Fallon spraying cooking oil down their lengths, he'd have torn off every piece. The flip-side seemed crisp and the steak aroma had him teetering on the edge of attack.

"Steaks are done. What about your skewers?" Warren lifted a heavy specimen off the grill. "This one might have to be yours. Janine's trying to slim me down this summer."

"I accept on behalf of me, myself, and I. These skewers seem past done. I mainly know how to test doneness with flakiness for fish, but the zucchini won't respond properly to that. They're too rubbery."

"Rubber, ash, and a little onion chocked in between. I'll eat two or three to destroy any evidence of overcooking. I've got your back if you've got mine."

"Yes, sir. Let me get these loaded and I'm right

behind you. Great job on those steaks, by the way. I haven't had a T-bone in years."

"Well, my baby girl is worth every ounce. Janine and I couldn't be happier that you two found each other. Now take good care of her for us. Let's get this food to the table." Warren led the way out of the smoke zone. The ladies waited on opposite sides of the table when they arrived with the platters. Warren served the steaks to individual plates.

He settled the vegetable kabobs like a centerpiece. Mirroring Fallon's preparations, he assaulted the bone with a knife blade.

Warren had no more sat down with his portion when Janine tapped her fork on her water glass. "Let's say the prayer first. And then I need someone to cut my meat, please. No more knives for me tonight."

Fallon chuckled and reached across the table for her hand. Court offered his beneath her free hand and bowed his head.

"For love, health, strength, and daily food, we praise your name Lord Jesus Christ, amen," Warren prayed.

"God bless the birthday girl," Court added. "May this be her year of greatest blessings."

"Thank you. It feels special already, even though Mom got hurt." Fallon released his hand belatedly as Warren stood to cut Janine's steak.

When she reached for the uppermost skewer on the platter, Court had to intercept with his fork. "Let me find you one from the bottom of the pile. I'll eat the crispy ones. Don't know what I was thinking about over there." He looked for a specimen that still had some color to it other than charred black.

"Daydreaming," Warren said.

"Too smoky to see," Janine replied.

"Here's the best one I can find." He passed the skewer to her and helped unload it from the metal stake with a wink. After putting two more unmercifully seared kabobs onto his plate, he found a healthy combination and landed it on Warren's plate. "Now forgive me while I execute my savage will on this T-bone."

"Go ahead, son," Warren replied. "No need to fuss about burnt vegetables when good meat is waiting. Help yourself, I'm right behind you."

Court took his first sumptuous bite. Juicy beef struck a direct hit on his taste buds.

"Dad, the steak is super. Great job." Fallon waved a piece from the end of her fork and Court trapped it like a frog catches flies, downing it before she could object.

Janine laughed. "I think you'd better get used to that grill before your corporate fishing fling gets started. We wouldn't want to make a bad impression on a paying crowd."

His mouth full of contraband steak, Court could only raise a finger in agreement.

Warren sat back suddenly. "Oh, good grief. It strikes me that I never turned that left burner down after I burned off the germs off. No wonder these skewers took such a dark tan. I left your side on roasting hot instead of medium high."

"Nothing bad came of it, sir, just a few onions crying from the edges."

"You two need to work on your team approach before we have to cook for seventy-five people," Fallon said. She gave him a furtive glance and dug out the center of her baked potato.

He knifed into his spud to let the steam out and freed several button mushrooms from the skewer. Warren leaned over to give Janine's potato a dab of butter. When she blew him a kiss in return, Court found the tenderness of their actions heartwarming.

Fallon's hand touched his knee under the tablecloth.

He leaned in to whisper in her ear. "I want this," he said, unable to stop the admission. Hungry in a new way, he watched her gaze soften until her lashes closed.

"Pass the salt, please," Warren said, nodding in his direction.

Court tried to recover and find the seasoning to no avail, though Janine rescued him with a one-handed reach for the shaker. Fallon giggled and held up another piece of steak, inviting him to take it, which he did like a barracuda. His feeding frenzy ran its normal course until nothing remained but a bone.

~

"You picked this out for me?" The box lid hit the floor as Fallon scooped out the salmon-colored wrap top and noted every detail that made it indescribably beautiful. A little fancier than most of her casual wardrobe, the pretty factor trickled into her heart.

Court nodded from his side of the chaise and locked his hands over his midsection. "Hold it up and let me look at you. I think it has the color of your hair in it." He reached out to touch her, but must have thought better of it. His hand returned to his side.

When she pulled the blouse in front there seemed to be some satisfaction in his eyes. "I've never met anyone like you in my life," she replied, breathless. She dropped the gift back in its box, but dared not stop looking at it—or she'd have to face him. Fussing with the tissue paper seemed safer.

His hand entered the neutral zone. "Come over here, birthday girl. You can explain to me how special I am from closer range."

She ditched the box on the end table to snuggle up next to him. "This is getting to be one of my favorite places. And the scenery doesn't depend on the weather. It's such a relief from being on the water." She folded her hands over his chest pocket and rested her chin on his shoulder, tipping up enough to be able to see his face.

"The support I'm getting from your folks is phenomenal. Make sure they know how much I appreciate them stepping in for the event." His lungs emptied and refilled.

She rode the rise like a near-shore buoy. "If I can keep Mom off 'self-destruct' mode, I think they'll do more than their part. She and I will tag team for the games and share the fun. Dad prefers kitchen duty. Will your folks come out for the fishing part? You haven't said much about their involvement."

"Carter's a maybe, but everyone else committed. Callie wants to help with the food service, and I think we'll need her help if all seventy-five people are going to eat at the same time. They're planning to ride out here together to save parking for the guests."

"Have them pull in behind the big house. It's more protected back there." She wiggled closer and tapped his chest with a finger. "I'm feeling pretty protected myself right now in Bait Crate Cove. What a great place to drift into for my birthday." A happy purring sound chased her confession as she closed her eyes to cherish his nearness.

He wrapped his arms around her and cinched it with a squeeze. "That song of God's deliverance for boaters really spoke to me, Fallon. I haven't had a chance to tell you how it sets my spirit on fire when you read to me like that."

She waited, sensing more to come. She searched his face for tender clues. They were everywhere.

"Something you said about 'when the lock gates open up to you' struck home, like it was something I was witnessing right in the moment. I've always held that it's a journey I'm on with this family business and with my life, standing one foot on land and one in a boat on the water. That often doesn't lend me a lot of traction to move forward, but that's changed ever since I met you. I get a true sense that the lock gates are opening up for me right now, and there's more out there than a horizon of water." He pulled her closer and gave her a long hug.

She couldn't have been more enthralled, birthday or not. His eyes had gone soft as the shallows in the lake, drawing her down. With one wiggle she could maneuver close enough to kiss him, but something made her wait, like surface refraction causes one hesitate before dipping the net.

"Fallon, when the lock gates open, what I see is love. It's sweeping me toward you in a current I can hardly fight. Not that I would even want to, but I have to make sure you want it, too. Can you tell me what you're feeling?" His hand found her shoulder, lifting her up so he could see straight down the canal of honesty into her eyes. One rebel finger traced her clavicle, stopping when it landed on her lace necklace.

When his thumb ran aground in the hollow of her

neck, the stroke of his touch unlatched a tremble from her core. What came up with it didn't have a name, but it rode on a bare shoulder. "I'm overcome with whatever this is, Court. I think about you all the time. When I paraphrased those words from scripture, I never guessed God would use them to draw two hearts together, but he has. If you're asking do I want you to see love when the locks open, my answer is 'yes.' I want you looking with love in my direction, because I'm feeling that way, too."

"I'm holding a blessing in my hands."

"What are you going to do with it?"

His thumb traced a cross at the base of her neck as his other arm brought her closer.

She allowed him to seal the declaration with an unspoken benediction. His breath became hers, a wondrous shared existence.

Chapter 12

Fallon stood at the bait shop door an extra second to savor the surprise she hoped to spring on Court. Since they hadn't planned anything for midweek, she could barely pass on the opportunity to come to town with Sheri and Liam to catch him off-guard. Impatient, she pulled the door open and stepped inside. "Would an interruption be welcomed at this late hour?"

Court greeted her with a smile. "I'm working on these food proportions for the big event. Every time I hit 'total' I think about you. Then you magically appear at my front door. Fancy that. I'll have to keep this calculator handy."

"So you know that I'm not a genie from a lamp, Sheri dropped me by while Liam is getting his braces fitted this afternoon. Guess that means I'm trapped here with you."

"I totally forgot about that gig. Did he seem happy about it?"

"Beyond happy. Sheri pumped him with anti-inflammatory tablets in case his mouth hurts afterward. He's a prime candidate for one of those before and after comparisons, that's for sure. Can I tell you how wonderful you are for doing that with your prize money?"

"Showing me would be better." He popped the calculator on the counter.

A noise rattled from the back room and a fishing pole fell through the doorway. "Uh, don't forget I'm back here." A middle school-aged boy appeared and retrieved the rod.

"Fallon, you remember Tanner from Memorial Day, right?"

"Hi Tanner. Glad to see Court's getting some help in here. Are things quiet around the neighborhood today?"

"Too quiet with Audie gone. Downright boring." He shuffled his oversized tennis shoes.

"Tanner's collecting loaner poles for me down the block and taping the owner's name on each one so we can return them to the rightful place. I'm holding the line on any extra expenses until we see how this Motorola group goes, so I'm cashing in a few favors to get these."

"How many did you collect, Tanner?"

"Sixteen so far. I haven't gotten very far down the street yet, though. We should be all right, if Mr. Reynolds brings in his poles, too."

"I like that 'we' you're using. Are you coming out to Loxahatchee for the fishing frolic?"

"Court asked me to lend a hand. Said it would be fun. I'm going to try to talk Audie into going with us, if there's room in the truck."

Court chuckled. "Oh, you know that girl. She'd strap

herself on top of the cab before she would accept being excluded. I think it's a given at this point."

"Hey, why don't you think about going horseback riding while you're out there? We could work you into one of the tour groups. There's an osprey nest in the cypress dome out back and you might even see some deer by nightfall."

"That'd be super! Maybe I could cut out while Court's cleaning the fish for dinner."

"Fallon can take your place, if Mr. McKenzie can lead the posse."

"That would be Mrs. McKenzie more than likely. Mom wants to split her time between games and the horses. She promised Mr. Nelson across the street that she'd keep an eye on his horses. That means I don't have to take out every group, so I'm happy." Fallon worked her way around the front counter to see what his calculations were adding up to for her menu.

Tanner cleared his throat. "Got anything else for me? I have the rods done." The teen glanced around the shop.

"What about feeding up for me?" Court asked. "You get started and we'll help with the back pond. Here's the key for the feed locker." He pulled a key from the top drawer.

"I'd like to see some of that action," Fallon replied, sensing the momentum shifting out of the room. A pinch on her side made her readjust her thinking. "Okay. See you in a few minutes, Tanner. Save me some feed."

"I'll get yours ready after I measure out mine. We don't waste anything here at Bait Crate. Court runs a tight ship." He disappeared into the back with a toss of his overgrown bangs and the screen door soon slapped shut.

"Come closer and take a look at these numbers. Does anything stand out to you? I've run through them twice now, so my eyes are starting to blur."

Unable to find another stool behind the counter, she hesitated. "Where can I sit?"

Court started to slip over and then opted for a different arrangement. He patted his thigh.

Exhaling like she really had to think it over, she alighted on the designated spot and directed her focus to the notations. "Half a cup of coleslaw per person is way too much. A serving spoon is approximately a quarter cup. Let's divide this total in half. Are you adding a cushion factor at the end? Round up your figure at the end, but keep your number at seventy-five for multiplying." She focused on the next column for the pork and beans, which was aided by a serving count on each can. A breath warmed her ear and the shop went from stagnant to steady breeze, neither too cooling.

"I think my bean estimate is solid." He blew a breath on her neck.

She giggled and brushed him back, trying to concentrate. "Yeah, I think we're good here. It looks like we should buy in bulk. Mom has a club card if you like the idea." Her finger traced the next column for hushpuppy mix. "This is more guesswork here, but if we overbuy, we can store the cornmeal and use it next time."

His hand tapped her hip and slid up to her elbow, searching for trouble. She trapped it against her side and turned to give him a corrective look. Anticipating it, he matched up to her in an instant and planted a quick peck on her lips. "I'm glad you think everything looks good here. Let me fine-tune these last adjustments and the list is yours."

"What fine adjustments? Do you mean estimating your tax?"

"No, ma'am. There's a handler's fee and I'm paying up front." Full of play, his eyes reflected a man who'd received his surprise visit quite well.

"I guess I'll allow it," she replied with feigned reluctance, turning toward him for the payment. The forty-five minute ride to town soon found its due compensation, as the shop owner paid with generosity for the extravagance of having his shopping list verified. She'd try to stay on the receiving end of that windfall more often.

"I love it when you're the surprise, Fallon. Catch me off-guard more often, I insist."

"Let's go feed those bait fish, so I can feel like I'm earning my keep." She took his hand and tugged him out the back door, laughing as they found the afternoon sun.

~

Court eased the boat off the dock at Sandsprit Park, letting Liam and Tanner jump ashore. Indian River Lagoon had turned aqua blue, making him glad he'd suggested the excursion. He strained to spot Fallon and Sheri along the shoreline on borrowed bikes, but couldn't make them out as the park use tipped the occupancy rate toward heavy. The aroma of hamburgers wafted off the land's edge and made him think of food for the first time. They'd have to wait and get something when they came back to Manatee

Harbor.

"Here they come," Liam shouted, his message altered by his new metal mouth appliance.

Court shut down the motor and drifted toward the steps at the dock's end. A pod of dolphins arched through the water near the inlet. He'd try to catch up with that marine mammal entertainment once the troops were on board. Fallon pulled up to the palm tree and locked the bikes. Liam and Tanner had volunteered to take the return pedal trip.

As the women walked up, it struck Court that Fallon wasn't as much a loner as she made out. With a little influence, she'd make a great connector, too. He waved and received a double greeting back as they stepped onto the dock. The boys rushed by, paused to horseplay near the ladies, and then threw themselves off the water side, landing in a big splash. When Sheri gasped, it fueled their boyish antics.

"I told them they could get wet before we headed out," he said. "I hope that's okay."

"The captain's always right," Sheri replied, heading down the stairs for the boat.

He extended a hand as she stepped aboard and then plucked Fallon from the second step, kissing her as she came aboard.

"Wow, I gotta find me some treatment like that."

"Oh? I didn't realize you might be in the market, Ms. Ware."

"Can't you see how she's melting down to nothing, Court?" Fallon moved into the bow. "Those are man-catching measures."

"You do look like a rail standing in the swamp, Sheri. Good for you."

"Fallon and I have a life-to-the-fullest challenge going on. My part entails jogging around the campground four times a day. I feel better eating right. Liam's even complaining about the lack of snack food around the house, but I think he has a hidden stash."

"As of today, no more popcorn or gummy bears for him," Court teased as the teenager appeared on the transom.

Liam shook his hair like a wet dog. "Are you talking about my 'no more fun' list?"

Tall and wiry, Tanner stepped in still wringing wet. Court pointed to the gunwale and the boy straddled it with a grin.

"I spotted a pod of dolphins heading out. We could make the passage with them if you two are ready." He flung a towel for their use.

"Ah, dolphins. I'd love to see them," Fallon said.

When Sheri stepped into the bow with her, Court took that as his signal to get going. The motor fired and Liam gave him a shove away from the dock. "One sunset cruise to the sandbar, at your service." The sun to his back, he turned his hat brim around and throttled up to accost the inlet channel.

Liam walked forward and soon pointed out the dolphin pod.

"Must be half a dozen," Tanner said. "Look, there's a juvenile on the inside."

"Oh, how precious." Fallon sat on her knees against the bow railing. "I forgot how magnificently they can carve the water. Look Sheri. The bigger one must be the mother."

"The big one's always the mother," she replied with a laugh. "Count them, Liam."

"Eight, I think, maybe nine."

"Look, there's more to the right as Manatee Pocket opens up," Court said. The sun glared on the water from that direction, but a merger with a second pod proved imminent up ahead.

Fallon clasped her throat as though she couldn't believe her eyes.

The entire scene became spellbinding. The boys shifted forward and stretched out on their stomachs, propping their chins in their hands to watch nature's show. The convergence happened in an arcing weave as the two pods merged.

Fallon slid off the bow and came to him, her eyes filled with emotion. "That coming together was the most beautifully orchestrated thing." When he shifted behind the console, she tucked in under his arm. "It's like a symphony of solidarity, such a meaningful movement." She nestled against him and gazed out to watch the dolphins work the channel.

"I love you, Fallon McKenzie," he whispered, "for how you see the beauty in the world, plus everything else that's tender and alive about you." He kissed the top of her head and her hair pressed against his lips like rain on a lightning bolt, invigorating and sizzling hot. Struck to the core, he spent the entire trip out to the sandbar with her in his arms, fused in the moment and woven together above a mist of marine blue.

Chapter 13

Fallon descended the tower's concrete steps Thursday morning to find Sheri punching through the steel door below. She looked like a woman on a mission.

"Your cell phone must be dead. Court called me so you would know that Carter's wife is in labor at the hospital. He sounded pretty excited."

"That man is all about family. Did he say anything else?"

"Only to pray for Tessa, as Carter said her attitude hasn't been too chipper."

"I'm starting to wonder if she isn't going through some chemical imbalance. Unfortunately, it's been manifesting itself as marital dissatisfaction. Wish I knew them better. Maybe I would have a better idea of what to recommend." Tired of her voice echoing off the concrete tower walls, she heaved the door open to a cloudless June day.

Sheri followed her out, something weighing on her countenance. "Father's Day is Sunday. It's not my favorite holiday, as my dad passed away and Liam's dad is not worth celebrating." Her mouth twitched like she needed to add something, but let it drop.

"Try making it your heavenly Father's Day. Do you go to church around here?"

"No. The campground sometimes has an informal gathering, but I haven't seen any interest for awhile. How about you?"

"I attend my parent's church most of the time, but sometimes I mix it up with cowboy church in south Loxahatchee. Not having all the trimmings of traditional worship comes as a relief every now and then."

"We could call ours 'fisherman's church' and be authentic. I'll see about getting someone lined up for the speaking part. Liam could find me some music."

"You might ask Charlie or Emmitt to come over and say a few words. They could take a break from the locks, depending on traffic. Or you could move the service onto the causeway between locks and make it easier for the working crew to participate." She dug her phone out of her pocket and confirmed what Sheri had already assumed. Her phone had no charge, a victim of last night's cruise. A sailboat motored into the open lock and she stepped away to give a hand with the lines.

"I'll go up and talk to Charlie while I'm thinking about it," Sheri said. "Let me know when the baby comes."

"Hey, would you take my phone up since you're going in?" Fallon pulled it out of the belt carrier and handed it to Sheri as she extended her hand with a smile. "Thanks for everything, Sheri. It helps to have a friend around here. It makes work more pleasant."

"Same here, Fallon. You're quite the motivational coach."

"When I'm not sidetracked by my bait fisherman." She exaggerated a wink under her sunglasses and turned down the lock.

"Oh, that the Lord would give me such a good-looking distraction," Sheri replied with extra emphasis.

Fallon chuckled her way to lock duty. At the upper bow cleat, she motioned for the line and the boater made a limp-wristed attempt to feed it to her. After more three tries, she snagged the rope and secured the vessel. Trying to better accommodate the senior sailor, she walked to the stern cleat and dropped to her stomach, holding out her hands for the line toss. When he outright dropped the coil, she rested face-down on the concrete flank and stared into the waters of the canal.

As the old-timer regrouped, a vagrant hand came to rest on her backside. She took an instinctive swat behind her, losing the freedom of her hand in an arresting grab. The despicable laugh let her know who it was without having to look. His grip on her back pocket wandered into a full-fledged grope. Her precarious position now compromised beyond tolerance, she yelled as she rolled sideways to break his trespassing hold and managed to reclaim her hand.

"How's my pretty girl today? Alive and kicking I see." Kit Rawlings righted his fisheries hat and moved his other hand to the top of her hip to pin her in place. The stern line landed across her shoulders and she grabbed it to gain traction.

"So help me, Mr. Rawlings, if you interfere with me doing my job, I'll have no other recourse but to report you to the district. Now make yourself scarce. There's nothing for you here." She elbowed at his last unwanted point of contact, ridding his touch though the repulsion lingered in her chest.

Rawlings stood, repeating his laugh. "Oh, there's something for me here, and I aim to get it." He spat on the ground and wiped his mouth.

Fallon ignored him and knelt by the cleat, wrapping the line in a figure eight to hitch it tight. She could hardly breathe. A shadow passed over her left shoulder and she looked up to find Charlie standing over her with the station's alligator rifle in his hands.

"I'll escort you off of Corps property now, Mr. Rawlings," Charlie said, his words measured. Led by the barrel, the fisheries officer relented with a final grunt of threat.

Fallon waved to the sailor below to let him know he was all set. Needing a distraction in neutral territory, she spied a fishing boat drifting too close to the second lock. With the pedestrian walkway open above the upper gate, she made her way to the grassy causeway flanking the spillway, and spent a few minutes calming down before she motioned them away from the "no fishing" zone. Two young men waved back and the boat soon headed downstream.

"God, please help me. I'm out here in a man's world feeling a little exposed today. You didn't make me fragile, but I'm going to need some help on this, or I'll be looking over my shoulder all the time expecting the next bad thing. That's no way to live, so I give this to you knowing you'll take care of me. Guard me against evil in the power of the Holy Spirit and in the name of Jesus Christ, amen."

She glanced around the familiar grounds and saw the trashcan's contents spilled across the concrete apron. Walking over, she pulled out the liner and tied off the top, dropping the sack to replace the plastic bag with another one stashed in the bottom. As she leaned over, she compromised her position again, the same way she did a hundred times around the lock every day. This was her job, so what else could she do?

~

The antiseptic smell of the hospital should have been a welcome change from the bait shop, but Court struggled to make the adjustment. The tile floors echoed every noise like a chamber leading straight into misery. Most of the occupants of the fourth floor hallway wore long faces as they sat in expectation. A sign led him toward the maternity ward waiting room and he took his hat off, combing his fingers through his hair. He recognized his father's stooped shoulders from behind and gave him a reassuring pat as he approached.

"Nothing yet. Not one word, plus, I haven't seen Carter in over an hour."

"Okay. Then I'm not too late to cheer you up. Where's Mom?"

"In the coffee shop. She must be reading the whole newspaper because she's been gone for awhile. I'm gaining gray hairs faster than grandbabies at this point. Did you call Fallon?"

"I finally got her friend Sheri at the campground. She promised to relay the news. Guess Fallon's phone needs a charge." He sat beside his father and scanned the magazine stack.

His eyes sparkled a bit. "Keep her out late last night?"

Court recognized a safe sideline for their conversation. "I took a boatload out to the south sandbar to watch the sunset. Sheri brought her to town for the orthodontist appointment I set up for her son Liam."

"I hear precious metals are a good investment these days. I'm proud of how you try to look out for the underdog in the crowd, son. Most people are all about self, but not my oldest boy. How'd you come by that? You didn't get it from me."

"Some from you, Dad," he replied, rocking his shoulder into his. "You never missed a chance to help somebody out—not that I saw. And maybe some of it comes from my heavenly Father. When his shoulder nudges me, I pay attention." His father's laugh mingled with the sound of a squeaking door. He turned in his seat to find Carter making his way down the hall. From his disheveled appearance, he must have spent the last hour in a meat grinder, not coaching labor. He tapped his father's shoulder and stood to greet the new father.

Carter stood a good three inches shorter, making his vantage point superior. Court had never seen a man fall apart before, but when every feature in his brother's face began to quiver, he thought he might. A breath catching in his chest, he tilted his head to ask what wouldn't come out of his mouth. In an instant, Carter's hands clutched for his shirt as his knees gave out. He crumbled in front of them.

A woman yelped down the hall and his mother came running. Court managed to pull Carter into a chair. An explosion of tears marked the wreck scene next. This wasn't the happy-father-delivers-the-good-news scenario he'd been expecting.

His mother knelt in front of them and his dad connected with his arm across his brother's back as he heaved and rocked to deal with the outcome. She produced a tissue, but Carter was too oblivious to take it, so she mopped the deluge on his cheeks for him, clucking with sympathy. Minutes passed and despair soaked into the group as Carter's laments radiated down the hall unabashed. Details of the story would come out in the end, but words would only cheapen it from here. Something had taken an unexpected detour south. It hurt more than Court could say. He'd have to look for God's hand in it somewhere, but right now there was only pain for the Reynolds clan. Pain and no gain, they had no precious newborn to celebrate today.

~

"I could transfer you up to Port Mayaca lock, but you'd be just as vulnerable," Charlie said, staring out of the tower's plate glass. "Rawlings runs the canal three or four times a week."

Fallon finished completing the blank on the harassment form and looked up to gauge her supervisor's concern."I haven't thanked you yet for bringing Old Swampy out to my rescue. Was it loaded?"

"Loaded and near 'bout discharged," he replied, his gray eyebrows cocked for good measure. "It wouldn't take much to send him reeling, not when he comes on you like that. Nothing good can come of it. Have you taken firearms training yet?"

"Yes sir. I'm certified to carry, but I'd prefer not to. My dad believes you're a magnet for trouble when you carry a gun on your hip. This seems more like harmless bullying behavior to me. He's stronger and he's taking it out on me. Maybe he likes to see me squirm." She stood and handed him the incident report, breaking his gaze over the canal run.

With some reluctance, he took the clipboard and scanned the report. She reclaimed her cell phone from the charger and started out, halting when his weathered hand hooked her arm.

"I'll let you by this time, but if it happens again, Fallon, I'll have to ask you to wear a weapon. I'm not a young man anymore, and my rescue pace has barnacles all over it." A weak smile appeared and he patted her arm as though to put the offense behind them.

She placed a hand over his in acceptance and then stepped toward the door. After all, there were locks to fill and boaters to assist with the crossing. She snapped her phone in place, hoping it would ring.

~

Court sat on the back steps at his father's house, his face hurting from the emotional punch-in-the-nose the stillbirth brought with it. Carter collapsed across his parent's kitchen table as his mother tried to mollify her questioning grandchildren. A nearby mockingbird sang against the sunset, its complex song warbling from one pattern to the next. The strident notes seemed to hold him to the earth. Glancing out at the dock, a strange detachment settled on him. The water didn't matter to him anymore.

Manatee Pocket already sat in shadows as the sun had set on the front side of the house. The darkness perched beside him and nothing seemed light. The hurt filtered too deep and offered no way out. He moaned and searched the familiar landscape for God, but found no signs. Restless, the bird flitted away and let the night come down like a ton of sky-bricks. Nothing splashed through his trance until his back pocket pinged. Producing the phone, he found a text that read "It's sunset." Knowing he needed to make the call, he forced his fingers to comply. "Hey. I need you, too. Sorry not to call. Things have been upside-down here."

"Any news about the baby yet?"

"No baby, Fallon. It came stillborn. Died in the birth canal, the doctor said. Carter's torn up beyond words." He rubbed his dry eyes as his tear-tank had run out hours ago.

"Are you okay?"

"Oh, I'm a bit out of joint. We're over at Dad's house. I came out back hoping the water would speak to me, but I'm flat-lining in the connection department."

"I'll pray for you all. Try to get some rest and let Carter know my heart hurts with him. Trust God with the hard things, too, Court. He'll make himself known, given time."

"Could you read something to Carter from your Bible? Maybe it would help him focus upward while he's in the valley."

"Sure thing. Let me run upstairs. Can you put the phone on speaker? I'd like you to hear this, too."

"I'll go inside and tell him what you're doing. Hold on." Court pulled the screen door open and stepped to the table, placing a hand on his brother's limp shoulder. "Carter, Fallon wants to read us a verse or two from the Bible. Should I bring the children in with Mom?" When his tousled head nodded, Court placed the phone on the table to collect the troops. With a finger pressed to his lips, he led them in until they flanked Carter on each side. His mother sat across his father's lap so he took the empty chair opposite them, bracing his chin on his palms.

"Hey everybody. Wish I could be there to hug you all, but I'll settle for this scripture about the opposite sides of life. Are you ready, Court?"

"Thanks for the hug. Go ahead, Fallon." He reached out and placed a hand on his brother's arm and his dad tethered the other side.

"A pendulum swings for every phase of life, from one side to its extreme:

birth to death,

planting to harvest,

snuff out to resuscitate,

demolition to construction,

crying to laughter,

intense mourning to jubilation,

scattering to gathering,

hugging to hands-off,

attempt to abandon,

retain to relinquish,

cutting apart to taping together,

quiet hush to eloquent speech,

tender endearment to spiteful estrangement,

engagement for battle to mutual truce.

"The hand of God sets the pendulum in motion. Thus, everything is made beautiful under the sway of time. With eternity set in our hearts, humankind can only wonder about the timeframe of God. Yet within each jeweled movement that elapses, we must find satisfaction in every work, as the moment is a gift of God."

Only silence trailed behind the resonating words. Court reveled that God had been there all along. The pendulum swing plunged toward the valley side right now, but God held firm, still centered on his throne.

"I think we're in the quiet hush part," Court said, squeezing his brother's hand. The squeeze passed to his father who hugged his mother. "Let me call you back later tonight, when my head hits the pillow."

"Goodnight and I'll be praying for you all." She made a sniffle before Court could hit the end button and let silence reign once again.

"Does the pendulum have a knife blade attached?" Carter asked, looking up at him.

"Probably, from the way it feels right now."

"Good thing he's a God of mending up the cut apart, like Fallon read," Jim added.

"He might run out of bandages and tape with me," Carter replied.

Court glimpsed a flicker of light in his eyes and gripped the back of his neck, giving it a brotherly shake.

"Grandma? I'm hungry," a child meekly said.

 Liv chuckled and brought Nikki to her chest.

"And Daddy's hungry, too."

"Maybe dinner is a good idea, honey. Will you help me mash the potatoes?"

Court looked over to the counter to see her pressure cooker in its spot on the back burner. Comfort food might be part of the pendulum's backswing to normal, mashed and lumpy.

~

Fallon didn't want to admit that waiting for the call had weighed more on her like being ostracized from the Reynolds family than a delay of circumstance. Had she thought of others first, it might have occurred to her that the delay came laden with bad revelation. Disappointed with more than her isolation, she walked the loft floor and glanced at the clock. Strewn with the fishing frolic food order, she stopped to make some sense of her desktop. They had a week to work past this and find their smiles, as the entertainment business didn't thrive on sad faces and dour dispositions. Her phone rang and she lunged across the bed as a shortcut to catch it by the second ring. "Hey, Court. Are things settling down now?"

"For me, a little. Carter's starting to pull out of it, too, I think. Your words tonight sure helped. We had a nice meal together and Carter returned to the hospital. They want to keep Tessa at least through tomorrow. She's pretty heavily sedated. Really, I can't talk about the hospital much more."

"One more thing and then I'll change the subject," she replied. "I keep having a hunch that Tessa might have some hormonal imbalance brought on by the pregnancy. Could you ask Carter to request a blood panel? Her doctor should see the wisdom in it. Catch him early, before she has anything to eat."

"She's refusing to eat right now, but tomorrow is a new day. I grieve for them both, as coming home empty-handed has a hollow ring to it."

"As hollow as being this far away from you." She hoped he felt the same.

"I fell out of love today—with the water. Manatee Pocket flat-lined on my register and I couldn't find the grace of God anywhere." His voice sounded shallow.

"When you're motoring in the valley, you can't usually see the water. Pull your boat into the lock of God's sheltering love and he will lift you up."

"Can you come to town for the memorial service, Fallon? I need to see you, to hold you. It's Sunday right after the eleven o'clock church service. We're at First Baptist, the tall steeple by the river east of the Roosevelt Bridge."

She closed her eyes and fell back onto the bed. "I'll come for both." They would climb out of this valley together, even if she had to drag him. The updraft of angel wings wouldn't hurt, either.

Chapter 14

The huge sanctuary supported two sets of stained glass windows, distracting Fallon in both directions. The pastor ended his sermon and requested prayer. Court bowed while Carter folded in half further down the pew. Through her lashes she saw a weathered hand drape across the heartbroken father's shoulders to comfort him. The sermon had been on the shallow side, promoting prosperity for the obedient. She didn't remember prosperity being one of the fruits of the Holy Spirit.

Her mind failed to track with the prayer as worship winded down to the last line item on the order of service. Too much pain resided on her pew for a regular Sunday morning message followed with a halfhearted prayer. They needed a real word from the living God, something that sank in and meant more than Sunday-go-to-meeting rhetoric. Hopeful for the memorial service, she'd bide her time.

Court glanced over at her after the benediction had

been spoken. He seemed beat up on the inside, his eyes bruised brown. When he touched a finger against her knee, she took his hand in hers. Maybe that would hold the hurt back. An organ struck a sharp chord and members of the congregation rose to go on their merry way. Restaurants would soon fill with the holy patrons and Florida's Sunday would remain bright and carefree, except for those staying behind.

"Carter's Sunday school class will attend the memorial," Court said, standing to stretch his legs. "His teacher volunteered to lead the service. Lance drives a bread truck before the crack of dawn every day, but he sure lives for the Lord."

"I'm a little overwhelmed in here," she replied, her gaze tracing the arch of the high ceiling. She slid from the pew and stood with him.

"Mom and Dad were married here. So were Carter and Tessa. I introduced those two. She attended my career class." He lowered his voice and spoke through her hair. "She kept adding an unspoken prayer request to the pass-around list, so I figured she might be looking for a good man." A fragile grin broke with the admission and faded.

"And Carter came to mind?"

"He hadn't made too many great selections on his own so I figured, why not? Eight months later I'm standing up front there, serving as his best man."

"Call that a different swing of the pendulum between that day and this."

"By far. Sorry you have to be here for the ebbing part, but I appreciate you coming."

"I'm here for you—and for the family." She fiddled with the strap of her purse while an elderly couple gave their condolences down the pew.

"Callie wants to come over to my place and work on her wedding invitations later this afternoon. Can you stay in town and help? We could have some alone time after that."

"Around sunset? That sounds like something I've been dreaming about. Sure, I'll stay." A group of young couples made their way up to the pew and began to settle in, all on one side of the aisle. That chopped the cavernous feel off the sanctuary and resembled a close-knit community a touch more. Several children ran across the narthex behind them as if launched from a slingshot. They appeared beautiful and full of life. To separate them from the memorial service would have been wrong. When three young girls brought Nikki and little Cayden forward, she sighed in relief.

Court sat and pulled the toddler into his lap, wrapping him in a bear hug. The boy resembled his mother with wavy hair and high cheekbones. When Fallon made a spider crawl across the plains of his shoulders with her fingernails, he ducked his head into his uncle's neck. Court nodded to the front platform. "That's Miss Jeanie, Mom's great aunt."

A white-haired woman wearing thick hose and shiny eye shadow placed a solitary floral arrangement on the stage. Studying its asymmetric shape, Fallon realized the white spoon mums were spilling out of a baby's bunting of some sort. The symbolic use of the utilitarian baby gear pricked her heart. A gold sash spelled out "Grace."

"If we weren't Christians, this would be impossible to accept," she said. A mild-mannered man took the platform and laid a hand on Miss Jeanie's shoulder.

They both nodded and she exited the stage, finding a solitary place on the front row.

"Tessa's here," Court replied. He stood with Cayden and made his way past her toward the front side door where the woman lingered, comatose in her countenance with dark circles under her eyes. He allowed the boy to kiss his mother, but held him back from the transfer of possession the child wanted. Carter drew closer and took her hand, leading her to their designated seats beside Miss Jeanie on the front row. Liv released Nikki and the girl took her place beside her father. Court sat by Nikki holding the youngest family member in place.

"On behalf of the Reynolds family, let me say thank you for staying today." The teacher pulled a slip of paper out of his Bible. Jim and Liv scooted down the pew to sit with her. Fallon reached for the hand Jim offered and saw him link with Liv on the other side. Callie and her fiancé Brian came in from the middle aisle and sat on her other side.

"Where, oh death, is now thy sting? Where your victory, oh grave?" Lance asked. "These are the questions that would haunt our lives, were it not for the resurrection of our Lord Jesus Christ. Today, we come to lay to rest little Grace Reynolds, who came to us conceived in love and flourished but a short time in the sole companionship of her dear mother."

Carter sniffled during the pause, so Jim leaned forward to donate his folded handkerchief. Tessa remained stoic, staring at the floral arrangement with the baby drape. Fallon's arms began to ache for a resisting weight so she crooked her elbow as if to nestle an infant within it. She had never given serious thought to rearing a child. Such co-dependency came to her as foreign. Court turned sideways and she studied his profile in a different light. Cayden's sun-bleached locks glistened against his chin. The irony of the innocent being taken hurt her heart as the boy's cherubic face shone. Peace on earth should never feel this laden.

Lance cleared his throat. "Jesus told his disciples 'suffer the little children to come unto me, for such is the kingdom of heaven.' And so today, we allow little Grace to rest in her heavenly Father's arms at his divine bidding." Carter choked on his grief and began a coughing fit that the speaker had to wait out, which he did with a look of compassion.

Miss Jeanie slipped out of her seat and knelt in front of Carter, patting his knee with her bent hand and whispering reassurances to him. Court moved an arm around his brother's hunched shoulders and Cayden reached for his father with dimpled fingers. A slender woman came and sat with Tessa, her eyes teary.

The family scene in front of Fallon began to overwhelm her self-control. Impossible to detach from, she allowed the service to include her, penetrated by the realness in this corner of the otherwise hollow space. Life unfolded here, with Court and his family. The ache in the crook of right her arm became more acute, so she cradled her purse. Jim squeezed her left hand.

"I'd planned to ask Carter and Tessa to come stand with me for prayer next, if they think they can manage." A shuffle on the front pew ensued as helpers walked the couple up beside the speaker. Court claimed Nikki in the void of their departure.

Fallon ventured a glance and saw him in a fatherly role, two kids in his clutch and love surrounding his being. A longing rippled through her, rocking her core and sending a shiver down her spine. Her shoulders must have shaken, as Callie placed a tender hand across her purse-hugging arm. Turning to nod her gratitude, she found the devoted sister had tears welling in her eyes. Lifting her free hand, Callie took it and interlaced her fingers. The strength of the bond simmered the prick of hurt.

"Heavenly Father, as we yield Grace to you, may your love be all she needs from this day on, as she sits in your presence with the rest of the innocents. We pray for Carter and Tessa, that in your mercy, their love would be somehow strengthened through their loss. We don't understand your rule of the great reversal, Lord, but Jesus taught us the last would be first and the servant would be the master. We release this infant to you and claim your promise for an abundant life, including this period of sadness that will lead to tears of joy some fine day. In the powerful name of Jesus Christ we pray, amen."

When Lance wrapped both parents in a circle of love, Court reached back to her. Jim placed her hand in his while Nikki, freed from her tether, darted to the platform. Liv broke forward next, hooking Cayden in her permissive arms as she went. Jim followed her up, but Miss Jeanie beat him there. Members of the class went up two by two, offering their personal condolences as Brian and Callie slipped out of the second pew to stand near the front.

Orphaned except for Court's hand, she allowed him to pull her to her feet where a hug across the pew started in Christian solace. Her shoulders trembled again and he tightened his grip. The wooden hymnal rack dug into her thighs as she slung her purse down on the pew cushion to take him fully into her arms. He buried several sobs into her neck as his breath became labored, his chest heaving against hers. Glimpsing the individuals on the platform, she noticed the bandage over Tessa's forearm and a blood bruise that trailed past it up a vein.

"God will tape this back together, Court. Trust him for today. Remember what comes after the pendulum swing of relinquish? We get to retain—which offsets the loss." She lifted his chin to quell his grief with her sincerity and gazed deep into his eyes.

"Help me get past the letting go—because it feels like I'm unraveling somehow," he whispered. His face resembled a question mark, contorted in grief with an open-mouthed poked at the bottom.

"Between God and me, we are not going to let you unravel. You may have to take him out of that tiny tackle box you think he fits into and let him be God of the universe."

"But that's my brother…"

"And God loves him more than you do. His fix will last longer than the Reynolds rigged-up approach, I assure you." Her revelation came followed by a slight smile and a coy look that melted into a slow wink.

The pressure from his hands lifted off her shoulder blades as his thumbs stroked her jaw line. "Can't imagine you not being here with me for this," he replied, looking like he wanted to kiss her. "Stay with me." His eyes begged for what his words could not as his fingers caressed her hair.

"I'm staying." As her face found his chest, she closed her eyes and blocked out the grieving throng.

After all, a time existed for tender endearment, so she accepted the moment for love among the aching.

Chapter 15

Court regarded the paper mess and wished the letter carrier would come and pick it up just like it was, without the fuss of preparation. He tried to get support from Fallon, but she had fallen too deep into her assigned task. Instead, he sat off the end of his breakfast table waiting for the next entry to make it through the chain.

"Anyway, the bridesmaid's dresses are a color somewhere between pink and peach—like the lining of a whelk shell," Callie said, the sweep of her hand scripting a flourish on another envelope.

Fallon took the combo stack of invitation and RSVP card, stuffed them into the addressed envelope, and slid it toward him.

In two swipes, he shellacked the seal and turned it over to affix the postage. The last stop came full circle, as the invitation ended up in the same box it came from the printer in, a true engineering feat.

"Liv told me her dress is the color of champagne." Fallon said. "That sounds rich."

"I'm trying to fight off the color war in the group pictures. This photographer is picky, but my only caveat was that he had to be invisible during the ceremony. Sometimes these things can seem a little… orchestrated. I want the wedding day to be about Brian and me."

"As it should be," Fallon agreed. Another envelope came at her and she had a handful of stuffing waiting to fill it up.

Court tugged at it prematurely hoping for some playful response. "I'll be invisible in black," he teased, taking the envelope. One hand slicked down a pretend lapel which garnered a surprised look from Fallon.

"Brian wanted black, so I caved. The shirts are white with a rust-colored cummerbund. It blends with the coral pink color, yet keeps it masculine." Callie finished addressing the next invitation and slid it across the table. "Nikki's dress is adorable. I can't wait for you to see it. The lace bow in back spreads to look like a butterfly's wings."

"That sounds darling. Will Cayden be the ring bearer?" Fallon's brow shot up with the question.

Court looked at her with admiration. "I'm still working on that one," he replied, an impish grin verifying it. "Callie wants an absolute guarantee that the boy can do the work, so I've got him in training. We have a practice pillow and everything."

"I wouldn't call that stuffed fish a practice pillow," Callie replied, restraining a smile.

He crowned her with his last sealing job before tucking it into the box. "No confidence in my influence, huh?"

"Seeing is believing. We'll have him suited up for

the benefit of the pictures, but he'll have to nail it at rehearsal to win the ring bearer job at the main event."

"Oh, ye of little faith," Court replied, nodding at Fallon. "See what insubordination I've had to put up with all these years? And Carter is worse." He reached for an envelope and she patted his arm in sympathy. After he swiped, wiped, stamped, and stuffed it, he gave his sister a loving punch in the arm.

Her pen trailed off the edge of the paper as a result and she grimaced.

"Uh, that one can be mine," he said, trying to take it from her.

She fended him off and finished lettering the script, then took the invitation from Fallon's hand and stuffed it inside.

"Straight from the bride and no stamp necessary," Callie offered. "Please come—and not because my oldest brother is a mess-up. Come because you feel like family and we wouldn't want to be apart on a wondrous day like this."

"I'd be honored to attend," Fallon replied, clasping the invitation to her chest.

"Great. Now I'll *have to* shave twice on September first."

"I already told you, Court—no GQ beard shadows just because the wedding's late in the day. I want clean and classic."

"Can I help with anything at the reception? I can ladle punch with the best of them."

"Thanks, Fallon. That's Miss Jeanie's department. I'll tell Mom and try to get you in."

"You make the Reynolds clan out to be some highfalutin club, little sister. Truth is, Dad won't speak to half his kinfolk, and the rest he doesn't claim."

Callie reached over and put the lid on the box and tossed the pen into her purse. "That's why the three of us have to stay close, Court. It's important that we don't stand by and let Carter's family crumble right before our eyes."

Fallon leaned over the table. "Is Tessa part of the wedding?"

"Tessa won't commit. I'm not saying that I can guess her motivation, but she gained two dress sizes with this third pregnancy. Maybe she's too self-conscious to be up front."

Court placed a hand on her knee below the table to connect. "I have a feeling her dissatisfaction goes a lot deeper than how she looks."

"Regardless of the reason, we should pray for her. I'd be glad to do it right now, if you can spare a few more minutes." Fallon looked across the table with a hopeful glance and Callie folded her hands in prayer, her engagement ring casting sparkles as it played the late afternoon sun.

"Let me end it, Fallon, if you'll start," he insisted, sliding his fingers onto her palm.

"Sure," she replied. "Dear precious Lord, we lift the Reynolds family to you as they plan the next family event and ask you to heal the hurt, especially for Carter and Tessa. Bind them together in love, dear Father, and help us be supportive in every way. Empower the doctors to help Tessa with her recovery and mend any rifts in their marriage, as only you are able."

"Yes, Lord, and I pray that our wedding plans don't pour salt into any wounds between Carter and Tessa," Callie added. "Help this to be a joyous occasion for all concerned, down to little Cayden. In some ways we're all toddlers, unsure of our next step. Show us the way under your will and help us walk the path each day."

Court squeezed Fallon's hand. "We allow you to be a big God from here on out, and give you the honor and glory for it all, in Jesus' name we pray, amen."

Callie stood and cradled the box in her arms. "Now I have to go check a few more things off my list." She headed for the front of the house.

Court followed like a good host to say good-bye at the door.

Fallon grabbed Callie's purse that had been left in the extra chair. "We'll walk you out and see if it's cooled off enough for a bike ride."

He opened the door and Father's Day heat hit him right between the eyes. June could be brutal this far south on Florida's peninsula, and it was delivering full force today. His polo shirt started sticking to his skin halfway to Callie's SUV. Maybe he could lighten up his attire before the next phase of recreation. Fallon passed him and placed the purse through the lowering window as Callie aired out the vehicle.

"Thank you both," she called. "Have a nice evening together."

Motion up the driveway caught his attention and his teeth clenched when he saw his next-door neighbor heading straight for them.

Deidra removed her cell phone from her chin and a complex look darkened her eyes. "Hey, Court. Got a minute?"

"What's up?" He pulled Fallon tighter beside him so there'd be no mistaking he had plans. Annoyance tainted his attitude before she got another word out.

"That was Kiera calling. She can't find Audie," Deidra replied. "She left her on Jupiter Beach to go pick up some fast food for their dinner. When she came back, Audie had packed up her beach stuff and was gone. I'm not worried she's drowned or anything. She's probably wandering around lost, trying to find her way back to Kiera's apartment. I was supposed to pick her up tonight anyway. Think you drive down behind me and help us search for her?"

"What about asking the lifeguards?"

"Or the Jupiter police?" Fallon added.

"No authorities, if we can help it, guys. I already have an HRS case file, and I can't afford any more incidents this year. Help me keep it on the down-low if you can."

"I'll go help—but only for one complete sweep of the beach and Kiera's neighborhood. If we don't find Audie, we go straight to the police before nightfall," Court said. "Agreed?" He held his ground as his neighbor squirmed, but he wasn't about going to waste his time under her undisciplined conditions. Fallon dropped her arm from around his waist.

"All right. By nightfall, we'll get the police involved." Deidra gestured with melodramatic flare. "That kid's going to be in so much trouble for all the aggravation she's causing me."

"You sent her down there, so now you have to bring her back. You're her mother."

Deidra shrugged. "I need to get the other kids buckled in, so give me a minute."

"I'll go find my truck keys and lock up the house." He searched Fallon's face. "Want to ride with me or drive separate?"

She scanned the sky as if searching for clues. "I'll drive down and meet you in the parking lot. Maybe we can enjoy sunset from the banks of the Loxahatchee River after everything settles." Her eyes held a flicker of hope.

"*If* it settles before sunset." Audie's face flashed to mind and it needled under his ribs. She'd forfeited his buddy system mandate, another grand lapse of his influence around here.

~

The sun approached the distant horizon as she stood on the dune crossover. Fallon knew that the search should have been resolved by now for the amount of manpower being poured into it. That assessment left her with one conclusion—things were about to get complicated.

Court stepped out of the men's changing cabana and shook his head.

"Whoever took Audie was long gone before we got here," she said, giving the beachfront another scan. Only a spattering of people remained, extending their weekend into the last moments of sunlight as the shore break tamed to a ripple.

Court backed against her and sighed, weary from his vigilance.

"Eternity must live in the ocean," she posed, trying to draw him out a bit. A line of retiring pelicans flew in a straight line headed south to roost. She counted nine and noticed a missing space between the last two birds.

"I saw the harbor patrol going by offshore a minute ago. Law enforcement is covering every angle which is wise, I suppose." Court sounded tired. He dropped onto the weathered wood bench flanking the platform and rested his head on the railing. "It's crazy what kind of thoughts can run through your mind with something like this. Everybody starts looking suspicious and my trust in mankind flies out the window."

"That's understandable, given the circumstances. Now you know what an officer of the law feels like. Charlie even wants me to start wearing my gun." She caught his inquisitive look, but decided not to bring up the latest Rawlings incident. "You know how drinking increases in summertime."

"Only because I see their lousy beer cans floating in the canal. Hey, I guess Deidra will be leaving at dark to get the kids back home. Want to come up with a plan for us?"

"Sorry to say, I've got to head out soon. We could stay until about nine, and then I need to go. Please don't feel like I'm bailing out on you, Court. Really, it's looking more and more like she's not here anymore. We need to let the police do their job. Abduction is a hit-or-miss creature. They need to find someone who's seen Audie with somebody else. Then we can narrow in on her whereabouts. Sitting here doesn't solve anything."

"But it's sunset," he said, turning toward her. She stroked his cheek and let her thumb rake over his bottom lip in tender promise. The sky color dimmed over the graying ocean and the faint cry of gulls crossed the dunes.

"Let's check in with Officer Gannon. I think I see him down in the parking lot. Maybe he can let us in on where the police are with fanning out the search." She stood and waited for Court to comply. He seemed willing, but his legs needed some convincing. She laced her arm around his waist and fused her hip against his like they were entering some ankle-tied relay race. Walking in step, they soon reached a small huddle of officers.

"Officer Gannon?" Fallon asked, waiting for his undivided attention.

"Mrs. Baines just left for home. I want to get both your phone numbers so I can contact you with any news." He took out a notebook and stood ready to record.

Fallon produced her cell phone and flashed the 'if found' file onto the screen. After several seconds, she brought up Court's number and shared it as well.

Court stood silent, his gaze drifting off into the darkness of the sea grape thicket.

"Are you at liberty to tell us where the police are with the investigation?" she asked.

"There are some complications with the search due to the number of homeless collecting just outside the park," the officer replied, his voice lowered for privacy. "We walked right into a small village we didn't even know existed."

"I work for the US Army Corps of Engineers and we find vagrants trying to set up shop on public lands all the time. Their shacks can be quite ornate as they pilfer items around the community. We even had one steal the shade cover from a fast food joint and was living under the candy-colored umbrella—quite a sight."

He regarded them and shuffled one foot in the sand. "The captain is planning a shake-down at dawn's first light. We have to arrange for the jail space ahead of time, or we'd have already run these fellas in. Once they're cleared out, we'll have the freedom to bring our dogs through and search for the girl."

"That makes for a long night for Audie," Fallon replied.

Court's gaze turned to stone.

Chapter 16

Being busy helped Court keep his mind off of Audie. Six pairs of grandpas and grandsons had already stopped by for bait on their way out to fulfill Father's Day promises to spend more time together, not bad for a Monday. He opened the spigot and aimed the hose nozzle at the deck of the fish cleaning station outside the bait shop back door. Heavily used over the weekend, he needed to check the honor system drop box for Sunday customers.

An incoming tide swelled the high water mark in Manatee Pocket as his gaze traced the familiar mangrove shoreline across from the shop. This edge of the continent had been his boundary for so long, he could hardly imagine what life might feel like not pressed up against it. Maybe not having tide charts and fishing tables would make life more even. He could stand some balance right now, as his scale had tipped toward the tragic and he didn't know how to level it aright. Fallon flashed into his thoughts, quelling some of his unease.

The rising sun pulled out of the treed horizon and cast long shadows from the Australian pines. Magnificent in its climb, the sunrise always shifted his thoughts to the spiritual. A new day arrived as God Almighty had ordained it. Was he enough of a believing man to accept its outcome, no matter how it fell?

"Lord, help my unbelief today," he begged. A crab claw crunched beneath his shoe, so he kicked it under the cleaning table. "Help Carter, help Tanner, and help Deidra. Everybody needs extra grace today, so please be generous. And look out for Audie, wherever she may be, amen." For once, the bait shop proved to be a safe haven for him. He shuddered at the thought of being down at Jupiter Inlet Park this morning. Officer Gannon assured him the police department would storm in at daybreak with their scorch-the-earth strategy for the homeless village tolerated for too long. Fallon held it was long past due, but hopefully not too late for Audie.

He bent to turn off the water supply and caught a motion out of the corner of his eye. Deidra's SUV backed out of her drive and hooked around to exit the neighborhood. A quick stab caught him in the ribs as the phrase "next of kin" popped into mind. Gannon had his number. Even though he wasn't blood kin, he presumed he might get notified if they got a break in the case. By the time he trotted up the back steps to close his distance to the phone, his knees started trembling. Not knowing amplified his anxiety. She could be anywhere.

~

"Finally came to your senses, did you?" Charlie nodded as Fallon stepped into the control tower. "It looks good on you—almost threatening."

She put a self-conscious hand over her weapon and checked to make sure it was secure in the leather holster. "Yeah, you don't want to mess with me anymore. I think I've lost my sense of humor."

"You're just a little bit savvier than last week—or scared." He turned with the day's activity chart in his hands.

She took it to deflect the insinuation. "Let's hold off on this trail maintenance until the first cool spell, at least a week or two when the rains come. I can start the dock work today. It won't be too hot first thing this morning."

"About the hand gun…"

"Court had a neighbor girl disappear on the beach in Jupiter over the weekend. Foul play is suspected, but she could be miles from Palm Beach County by now."

"I might have seen that on the news last night. Cute little thing, too. How's he doing?"

"Oh, you know. Court thinks he has to hold the world together sometimes, networking and pulling his deals to connect people. That openness leaves him vulnerable to hurts like this." She leaned in to glance up and down the canal. No vessels approached the locks, so she could start the maintenance right away. "Come down and get me set up for the dock resurfacing. I'll listen for your bell if someone floats into the lock."

"Guess I have to say 'yes, ma'am' now that you're packing some heat." He chuckled and opened the door for her to descend, quirking his expression to resemble Pop-eye.

"That's the kind of respect I'm after," she replied with dry wit. Some parts of this job were truly precious to her—but only some parts.

~

Well after ten o'clock now, Court anticipated Carter's arrival. He'd escorted Tessa to her mother's house for a couple of days of recovery and solitude. Liv would keep Nikki and Cayden through midweek so Carter could get back to work. He'd mentioned something about making the snack food pick-up, eager to see if the idea would float. Change could be good, Court assured himself, looking down at the paperwork for the first fishing frolic. In fact, he was hedging his future on it.

He stepped from behind the counter and selected a spool of midweight monofilament line to finish rigging out the loaner poles. That would keep him busy until his brother came in and he'd have the poles ready to deliver to Fallon. Since she intended to purchase her bulk supplies on Tuesday, maybe he could run the poles down to the cabin this evening.

The idea brought satisfaction with it as he let the memory of their cypress dome horseback ride replay in his mind. Only the osprey nest reminded him of the coast, all else was inland wonder. The sensation refreshed him as he reached for the first fishing pole whose eyelets were vacant. He would string this new venture together one implement at a time, and cap it with a tiny hook.

~

Fallon looked up to see the Fish and Game boat nosing away from the upper lock gates, trying to look busy. Too bad there weren't any fishermen nearby.

"What's Rawlings doing swarming around here like a vulture?" Liam asked as he helped sand the handrail down to the dock.

"He's pretending to do his job, but really he just wants me to turn around and validate him with some attention."

"I think you should turn around and flash him your new hardware."

She tried to shush him with a wave of her sandpaper. "I'd rather show him your new hardware. Your teeth are already straightening out, Liam. It's only been two weeks."

"That's what Mom says. She thinks I'm going to have a killer smile. I just want it to be normal, so I don't have to be so self-conscious."

"Do you have any trouble eating?"

"Mom's been cooking soft stuff like meatloaf and macaroni. I have to cut fruit up now, so no more monster bites. I still get plenty hungry, though."

"Sheri should crank up her blender. Smoothies would be good for you. Hey, are you making the bait fish run tomorrow around Lake O?"

"Yeah. Guess who I'm meeting up with? It's that Heather whose grandpa had the heart attack. She and her dad want to get the boat, so I said I'd help out. We're meeting at Jake's Fish Shack at four o'clock."

"Tell her I hope Mel is doing fine now. That gave us quite the scare."

"But at least you got to meet Court." Liam took one final pass with the sandpaper and let it flutter down to her at the bottom.

She snatched it up about the time a metallic click sounded over the water. It seemed the fisheries officer wanted to grace them with a comment, but no message followed. She stood and stretched the kinks out of her back, facing inland to ignore him.

"Go away," Liam yelled, motioning with a swipe of his hand.

Fallon turned to cut a final glare his way, but the stare-down approach didn't seem to faze him one bit. She would not respond further to his inane luring. Charlie rang the loading bell and she ran up the ramp to help secure the boat coming into the lock.

"Please move off the north gate," Charlie called through the megaphone.

She closed the distance to the lock and Liam ran up on her heels to lend a hand.

Rawlings must have taken the hint as his boat moved on up the canal to go be predatory on someone else.

"Tell Sheri that Rawlings is acting creepy," Fallon said between breaths. "I see her out here running in the morning, and I don't want her to be caught with her guard down."

"She'd scratch his blinkin' eyes out if he tried anything," Liam replied. A metal-laced smile validated the claim.

She had no doubt the reactive woman could hold her own. Hearing her holster squeak with each jogging step, Fallon began to enjoy the presence of her new sidekick. Her father called a gun the great equalizer. She hoped she never had to find out.

~

Court heard the vehicle door slam and tried to finish rigging the pole.

"Here's the snack man with the grand plan," Carter said, winging his way through the back screen door. "I'm going to set this up so irresistible, sales will be through the roof."

Court dropped the pole to grab some boxes leaning

from his stack. "If you say so, candy man. Just keep this stuff out of the bloodworm fridge, okay? Maybe we should wash our hands a whole lot more, too. How's Tessa this morning?"

"Quiet, but recovering. Lab work is due back tomorrow, but right now she has stitches in places that make it hard to get comfortable. I left her on the sofa at her mom's house with pillows under her knees." He sat four boxes on the front counter and levitated his hands over it as though testing for proper fit. Squinting with concentration, he chose to move two boxes of lures away from the register, handing them toward Court.

"I hope keeping your hands busy will keep your mind off your woes." Setting the food acquisition down, he took the cast-offs and stepped into the store to find shelf space for them.

"We talked a little on the way over this morning. I asked Tessa to give her unrest to God and take her time to come to grips with losing Grace. I'll be here for her when she pulls out of this. I vowed to God that I would the day we got married, and nothing's changed that." The first box popped open and cheese nabs appeared.

"When did my baby brother get so grown up?" Court pretended to reach for a sample. His hand got reprimanded by a fly swatter while the bug got away.

"Having a wife and two kids can grow you up real fast. Of course, there's nothing like the threat of losing it all to make you appreciate what you've got. I want my happy home back, filled with a loving wife and playful children."

"Way to fight for it, Carter. I'm warming up to the idea of having snack food around. Make it look good up here, and I'll ask the regular customers to partake when

I check them out."

"Hey, have you heard anything more about the missing neighbor girl?"

"Nothing. The police started raiding the homeless encampment at dawn this morning, but I don't know if it yielded any clues. When I think about the possibility of Audie walking right into that viper's nest unaware, my skin crawls."

"Don't torture yourself by assuming the worst, Court. I've been praying for you this morning. It seems we're both being put through the refiner's fire lately."

"I might need to get away from the heat by driving out to Loxahatchee this afternoon. Every time I look at that makeshift memorial off the end of my driveway, the dread amplifies. I'm too close for comfort here, but there's nothing I can do."

"Sure, go ahead. I'll close up" Another box flipped open, revealing short tubes of vanilla sandwich cookies. Carter looked up at him and smiled. "Remember our secret stash in the attic?"

Court ran his hand into his pocket and tossed his silver change onto the counter. "Yep. I'll go load the poles." He raked his hand through the box to snag a pack of cookies and left.

"Hey, big brother, want to share those?"

"Get your own, candy man." He punched the screen door open and scooped four poles inside the circle of his hands with the cookie pack wedged in his mouth, wrapper and all.

~

"Go ahead over to Sheri's for lunch while I've got Liam here," Charlie said, examining the sanding job on the dock. "He and I didn't get any time together for

Father's Day anyhow."

"That sounds good. Sheri's treating me to rabbit food with tiny shrimp floating on top. Liam, are you good for now?"

"Yeah, tell her I've got this dock work to keep me occupied, so she won't go hunting up something in the campground to make me earn my keep."

"I'll share my Vienna sausages and hunk of sharp cheddar with him when we take our break," Charlie added. "We can wait until you get back, so we'll have someone in the tower."

"I think we've had our pulse of pass-through traffic anyway. Be back in thirty minutes." Fallon dusted her hands off and searched the parking lot. A family of four retreated to their car after a full morning on the nature trail. The blond children seemed so precious and eager to explore everything. It's a wonder their handprints didn't decorate the newly refinished rail.

She opened her car to retrieve her lunch cooler, hoping the rice crackers and low-fat dip didn't tip Sheri's fairness scale of allowable dietary intake. What a pain to have to quantify calories. She didn't have time to live like that. A lot could be said for staying active.

She squeezed the door lock and made a beeline to the campground office where a whirring noise filtered through the screen door. Sheri sat on an exercise bike, creating a whirlwind with her pedaling fury. Fallon laughed and entered the lobby. "Can you fit me in? I only have thirty minutes." She raised the cooler to validate the claim.

Sheri came off her exercise circuit, setting the pedals free. "Girl time at last." She wiped her forehead with her shirttail.

Fallon spotted proof around her waist. "You really look great, Sheri. If I was dieting, I'd be hungry all the time. My strategy is not to think about food, and only eat what I'm hungry for at the time."

"Where were you twelve years ago when I ate my way through a divorce and Liam's elementary years?"

"In the high school cafeteria," she replied with a laugh. She rested the cooler on the counter and pulled her phone out to check her messages. None were waiting.

"Haven't heard back from Court yet about the girl?"

"No, too many unknowns at the beach. Let's hope she pops up in some convenience store with a tale to tell about her misadventures."

Sheri pointed at her weapon. "Is that your onion chopper on your belt?"

"How do you want yours—minced or diced?"

"No thanks. I've already got the salad made. Let's sit out back under the golden shower tree. There's a breeze off the canal today."

"Let me sit with my back to the water. We had a vulture hovering earlier, and I'd just as soon not know his whereabouts."

"Is Kit Rawlings eyeballing you again?"

"Don't make me have to admit it, but he's the reason for the onion chopper."

"Maybe Charlie should pull some strings to get him relocated from the St. Lucie canal. You know what I mean, the nuisance alligator treatment."

"Give me a reptile any day. Put a snout choke on them and you can lead them anywhere. Rawlings, I'd rather not touch."

"I hear you, girlfriend. Come on back and let's get

this lunch going."

"I brought the dip. Hope it's low-cal enough for you."

"I could splurge a little if you keep me entertained with fascinating stories about Court."

"Our big fishing frolic kickoff is this Saturday. He's super into the fishing aspect of it, and Mom is helping me estimate the food quantities. We're feeding seventy-five members of an employees' club."

"Maybe Liam and I could shoot over to help out. It's at your place, right?"

"That would be great. I could use your help with the meal and Liam could help the kids bait their hooks. If we run low on fish, he could even test his mastery out on the stocked bass."

"Ask Court if he wants the extra help. I've always wanted to see your log cabin."

"Liam wants to ride my horse. Would that be a problem?"

"Not at all. This is my summer of letting go."

"Wow. Who is this new woman?"

Sheri shoved the back door open and gestured toward the picnic table under the shade. "Half the mess she used to be. Life to the fullest means no more wallowing in regrets."

"I admire that. Looks like you're winning the challenge. You're becoming a fetching damsel while I look more like Marshal Dillon every day. It's a wonder Court even notices me."

"He's holding back because he's a gentleman, Fallon. Sometimes when he looks at you, it's like some gravitational force gets engaged. Wish I could have a polar opposite like that."

"Get yourself where you want to be and it'll happen. Now, let's get at that salad or Liam will be back over here after me. By the way, he said not to expect him around the campground. Charlie has him on task for the Corps."

"The old codger is finally ready to have that grandfather-grandson talk with him. He mentioned it this morning." Sheri sat facing the waterway and snapped the plastic tub of mixed salad open, sliding a bowl toward her. "You're a good influence on him, Fallon."

"I just try to live out the Christian life, one trial at a time."

"Say the blessing because I think God is listening to you." Sheri winked and covered the salad with the web of her interlocked fingers.

Fallon bowed, thinking they had more pests around than an errant fly, which gave her more reasons to pray.

~

Court fit the last three fishing poles into the rod holder and gave the effort a cursory inspection. Nearby, the scrub oaks resonated with the chatter of blue jays and a mockingbird called from the horse corral area. Peace lived out here, not to mention someone very special to him. Unable to sort the two apart, he accepted the buoyant sensation as a blend of relief. When he heard a car coming down the gravel lane, he wiped his eyes clear. Attempting a casual greeting, he waved and leaned on the open tailgate.

Fallon pulled up with her jaw dropped at the sight of him. In seconds, she approached with unsure steps, searching his face. "You're here to meet me? It's not about Audie, is it?" She pulled off her holster and locked it in the trunk.

He glimpsed the weapon, but wouldn't let it distract him now. He had to share the news without breaking down. "The police found a child's body this morning in a shallow pit under the sea grapes. Deidra made the identification around noon. It was Audie, no doubt about it."

"God help us," Fallon replied, reaching out for him.

With no ability to resist, he folded into her arms and squeezed her so tight, he thought she might complain.

"Poor sweet girl. I can't even imagine what she went through…"

Hard-pressed to reply, a sob wracked through him and his chest trembled. "They think she tried to take a shortcut off the beach to head back to the apartment."

"And she stumbled right into that pack of homeless filth. Dear Lord, no." Her fingertips began forming soft circles on his back.

Not trusting his legs, Court leaned back onto the tailgate and put his hands on her shoulders to take a long look. He'd never had anyone to share his sorrows with before. It had a remarkable feel to it, almost redemptive. His thumbs swiped the tears rolling down her cheeks. "I'm breaking in half wondering if I should have kept her around the bait shop more so Deidra wouldn't have farmed her out to someone even more negligent."

She touched his chin and looked deep into his eyes. "You cannot accept any blame for this, Court. It's beyond your sphere of influence."

Regret surfaced and overrode his anger. "So many people within arm's length, all those I want to reach out and draw closer."

"You do have that effect. Look at Liam. Look at Tanner. Those kids are drawn to you because you treat them like they matter. You make a difference every day."

He clung to her again, letting the grief drain from him as the mockingbird's soulful dirge brought down a heavy evening.

Chapter 17

Work shouldn't be this fun, especially in the wake of a family tragedy, but Fallon knew the look of pleasurable success and Court sure had it. She tied her reins to the handrail and indulged in watching him work with half a dozen youth lining the pond's shore. The lesson must have been how to set the hook, and immediately after illustrating the arm jerk motion, a teenager's pole dipped and he got to practice the technique. When a small bass flopped onto shore, Court clapped his approval and the kid simply beamed.

A photographer jogged over and captured the occasion as the boy refused help to remove the hook. In a catch and release moment, the fish glinted in midair and splashed back into its home. A challenge ensued as the surrounding youth caught fishing fever and adjusted their lines to increase their chances of getting a hit. By the time her last rider made it back to the barn, two more kids had fish on the line. As the rider dismounted, she recognized his green bandana as an affiliation with the accounting department.

"This outing is good medicine for me," he said, stretching his legs. He removed his sunglasses to wipe his face and she could read the earnestness of his admission.

"Sometimes work isn't enough, is it?" She took his reins, tied the horse next to hers and ran an appreciative hand down its sweat-slicked neck.

"No, you're right. There's more to life than spreadsheets and expense justifications. I won't have a hard time with this cost, in particular."

"Your company is our first group, so we'll be asking for input on your experience. The department games are next. That should be a real hoot."

"Send us an evaluation form by e-mail. I bet you'd get plenty of positive feedback. Unless you plan to burn the food, I can't think of anything that needs improvement. That shade sure felt good back along the cypress swamp. If you held this in the fall, the temperatures would be much more comfortable."

"And the fishing would be better, too. Good point. I'll make sure Bait Crate gets your suggestion. See you at the game course in a few." Fallon stepped toward the barn and returned his farewell wave when a cheering ruckus broke out on the pond's edge. She wandered back into view and saw the smallest boy with the biggest bass, a winning combination. Court wheeled a cooler closer and the photographer had them pose together with the fish. He knelt and clasped an arm around the boy's puffed up frame as she witnessed another bond being forged. Court was a natural father figure.

"Fallon, there you are," her mother called,

approaching at a fast pace. "Dad's ready to get the games going, so ask Court to make the announcement. Doug Nelson wants to help after he gets the horses put away, so that will free up your father to assist at the grill."

"Okay, Mom. I'll stop by and get washed up before there's a run at the hand-washing station. Oh, and tell Dad the accountant doesn't want the food to be burned, so the grilling has to be perfect." She drew her lips tight so her mother could appreciate the jab, which earned her a light laugh.

"I'll help get the kids cleaned up if you can prep the game area for the first event. Dad's expecting you."

"First, I need to rendezvous with my leader—even if he smells like a fish pond." Fallon broke into a trot to get the transition underway as the party unfolded before her eyes, individuals at their leisure all around her property, enjoying the natural beauty and the companionship of their work comrades. She stooped at the faucet off the front porch of the kitchen and slathered her hands with liquid soap. Drying them with a paper towel, she headed in Court's direction. When he received her with a big smile, she had to resist the hug she wanted to deliver. "It's time for the department games to begin."

He reached for her and must have thought better of it, his wrist flexing into a stop signal instead. "Let me give a one-minute warning, as we have a little man-to-man competition in progress here." He turned back to the pond and cupped his hands around his mouth. "Game time begins in five minutes over behind the barn. One minute left for the fishing contest, gentlemen. Get 'em on now or forever hold your peace."

A group of ladies clapped from the shady rim, driving his threat into higher gear. Two boys separated from the group along the pond's bank and tried their luck solo. Court collected several unused fishing poles and put them in the rack.

She flashed him a coy smile and rolled the rack higher on the bank. "Will we have enough fish to feed the multitudes?"

"These along with the ones your dad and I snagged yesterday should be enough, by far. Thanks for helping keep me on the timeline today. I want their experience to seem both leisurely and chock-full all at the same time."

"The comments have all been fantastic so far."

A boy called from the pond and revealed a nice-sized bass to add to his record. Court clapped and jogged over to help unhook the catch, followed by the ever-ready photographer. The ladies in the shade strolled down toward the barn, following the orange pennant tape her father had strung. More than looking festive, it felt genuinely pleasurable as she watched the kids return their poles to the rack. Spotting her mother at the washing station, she turned her attention back to Court.

He stood watching her. "Hope you have you're A-game on for this next part, Miss McKenzie. Mr. Shaw has asked Team Bait Crate to play in because they have an odd number of departments. I told him that would be no problem, even though we haven't practiced a lick."

"That should make it about even, don't you think?" The faucet squeaked open and a jet blast of water shot out at the first in line. She laughed as her mother hurried to adjust the pressure, offering a dollop of soap all down the line. Several hands immersed under the steady stream and the enthusiasm of their banter became contagious. Hearing the rack pull up behind the porch, she turned in time to see Court's admiration of the scrub-down scene. What an upbeat break from his downer neighborhood back in Port Salerno.

"Dad asked for help setting up, so I'll be off now."

"And I'll stay back and start the fish cleaning. Send word when it's our turn for the gunny sack race and I'll come right over."

"Good plan. I'll send Mom over when it's time. Don't let her near a knife, though."

"Oh, I wouldn't dare," he replied, a tease in his tone. He looked like his old self—or maybe even a touch better, like the colored haze a rainbow gifts to the sky after a severe storm. Happiness became her pot of gold, even if she had to wear a gunny sack to catch it.

~

Court walked into the roped-off game arena. "Don't start this last race without me." He saw several blue-shirted teammates and headed that way. Fallon stood alone at the starting line for the double-down dare of the three-legged race, waving the ankle tie at him like a lure. His competition craving notched up a level and he eyed the course distance as he jogged over. His sister and father teamed together next to Fallon while Warren held the flag to start the race.

"Hey, great idea for Team Bait Crate shirts," he said, taking the ankle tie and aligning his hip to hers. With his molecules already in motion, he hoped he wouldn't drag her down the run. "Don't let me leave you behind, lady of the locks."

Fallon tightened her ponytail. "This event is supposed to be an adjustment toward teamwork." Her arm dropped around his waist. Several green bandana-wearing individuals took their place along the starting line.

"I like my teammate just fine. I only hope she can get the move on, that's all."

"It wouldn't look right to beat your event customers, would it?"

Warren raised the flag, so he held his response. He wouldn't cave under the pretense of propriety, he'd simply offer a sporting pace to challenge the others. If Fallon could keep up, they'd be up front for sure. The flag snapped down and they stepped out on the banded middle leg, finding a rhythm with springy steps and an open stride. His sister laughed from behind and he forced the pace to ramp up their speed.

"You okay?" He glanced down to gauge their mechanics. He seemed to pull her stride a bit, but she made the adjustment. A green-banded team loped slightly ahead and he looked back to assess the field. "We need to speed up. Are you with me?"

"I think," she replied between breaths. Her grip tightened around his waist.

The gap closed up between the loping accountants and he felt they had a rough shot at the finish line ribbon. In a last pump of effort, he opened his stride. "Final kick," he said, which only seemed to motivate the green team off his right shoulder. As they jetted ahead, Fallon's ankle gave a wobble and her foot landed under his, taking the brunt of his weight. The stumble that came next occurred as the finish line broke across the green team. In seconds, all he could see was grass and strawberry blond ponytail. Fallon's laugh made the landing softer, and he managed to pull her back on top of him. They rolled with the momentum as his sister's ankles passed them by at a steady clip.

"Trying too hard, big brother," Callie called.

He watched from the ground as they came in second place. The rest was all green headbands in celebration.

Fallon flipped off of him and rested on the ground at his side. "Even disqualification feels good when I'm with you," she teased, still trying to catch her breath.

When he dug a finger into her ribs, she squawked like a kid, so he had to go back for more. The tickle-fest took a turn toward chaos when his junior fishing buddies piled on, wanting to join the action. He found a few more ribs, dug a few collarbones, and discovered Fallon was ticklish on her hips. The mob became a ruck of revelation and the photographer knelt in front to capture the impromptu images digitally. Exhausted and out of breath, he laid back and exposed his vulnerable core to the clan of boys who showed little mercy.

Callie came to his rescue and offered him a hand up while their father helped Fallon. "I finally beat you at something, so I suppose my childhood can come to a satisfactory end," she teased, brushing off his back.

"I hope so, since you're planning to get married at summer's end."

She held up two fingers, a reminder of his disqualified plight.

He nodded in humble concession, turning to find Fallon. She pulled off the tie and took her independence with a slight limp. Guilt came fast and hard. "Injury time out," he called to Warren, sweeping Fallon up in his arms. "Looks like you'd better skip us for the gunny sack race."

"Janine and I will represent Team Bait Crate then,"

he replied. "You kids go on up to the kitchen and get started on the fish."

Court strode into privacy behind the barn as Fallon clamped her arms around his neck. Worried that he might have overstepped in his enthusiasm, he looked down searching her face for some clue of her condition. The blush of her freckled cheeks somehow distracted him and when he found the liquid pool of her gray-blue eyes, distress gave way to caress.

Drawn to her, the kiss came without hesitation, lifting the frolic experience into the lower atmosphere reflected by the pond. He stopped to find the barn wood with his back, pulling her closer and magnifying the kiss. When she pushed away to catch her breath, he looked at her in wonder. Funny, she could make a loss vault into victory just by being with him.

She cleared her throat and nodded toward the kitchen. "We'd better get cooking, as that accountant who just beat us to the finish line doesn't want his food burnt."

"I'll show him my version of crisp," he threatened, kissing her nose but refusing to put her down. Maybe they could cook like this, though grilling might get tricky. Remembering her ticklish spot, he dug his thumb into her hipbone and she laid back into a full-throated laugh. What a happy man that made him, even if his pride had taken a fall short of the finish line.

~

Fallon scooped another serving onto the accountant's plate.

He tugged the green bandana to the base of his neck. "Could you give my wife your recipe for this coleslaw?"

"The secret ingredient is crushed pineapple." When the boy beside him turned up his nose, she passed on to the next family. Her mother followed with the last pot of baked beans and used a similar technique to try divesting them of any leftovers. Court appeared with one last platter of grilled fish and set it down in front of the big boss.

Mr. Shaw stood and clapped his hands. "My fellow employees at Motorola's Palm Beach Gardens division, I'd like to express my sheer delight to have you here on the inaugural outing for Bait Crate Fishing Frolics. If you've had fun today, would you please join me in expressing our appreciation to Court Reynolds and his support team?" The large man lifted his arms and applause echoed inside the kitchen. A few hooting calls came next as boys jumped up and down beside the tables. "And I don't think there's anything better than fresh fish off the grill."

This time a hoot came from the accounting section, led by her horseback riding friend. Fallon soon found the acknowledgment reflected in the look of gratitude on Court's face.

"Then I hope these lemon tarts won't go to waste," Jim replied, flourishing a tray filled with the treats. The applause started again while Callie fanned out to serve her tray to a host of children. Mr. Shaw offered Court his hand and they shook to seal the success of the day.

Fallon emptied the coleslaw bowl and traded for the fish tray, brushing Court with her shoulder to flash him an admiring look.

Mr. Shaw grabbed his fork and stabbed a crisp-edged specimen before she made off toward accounting, causing her to chuckle with satisfaction. "We'll start the award ceremony and hold our prize drawings right after I devour this fine fish."

Callie passed her with the tart tray and leaned in for a private message. "I haven't seen Court this happy in a long time. Keep him out here and away from the tragedy back on the block as long as you can. I know it's a stall tactic at best, but I think he wants to be waylaid."

"Dad invited him to stay out for church tomorrow. Seems everyone is plotting in secret."

"Not me," Callie replied. "I'm working with you. I even have a firm target to aim my bouquet at during the reception." She winked and stepped down the line to give the green headband people their dessert.

Her tray now empty, Fallon stepped over to the sink and dipped the serving piece into the sudsy water. Warmth flooded over her as her hands diverted to automatic cleanup duty. So Court wanted to be out here with her. She would unashamedly treasure every minute of it.

~

"Mr. Shaw gave me a bonus tonight. Should I attempt to pay your parents?" Court's eyebrows rose as he made the inquiry, sincere to follow through.

"They wouldn't accept anything." She placed the "God Be Near" pillow under her ankle. When he turned making the chaise creak, she tensed for no reason. "Why don't you pay it back to the bait shop? I'm sure you could cover Carter's new snack overhead."

He snorted in protest and touched her hand. "What could I do for you? I mean beyond pray for instant healing for the ankle injury I caused. I can't believe I did that all in the heat of competition."

"What you meant for selfish gain, God turned into priceless goodwill with a client. Not only did the accounting department earn merit in the eyes of their peers, a dust-cloud of little boys got to cherish their fishing hero with an impromptu tickle-fest."

"We showed them a good time, didn't we? And I really loved every second. It's hard to explain, but I never wanted it to be over. The award ceremony at the end was a fitting touch. We should recommend that to future clients, to lend us a grand finale."

"The color-coded department teams and the photographer both turned out excellent ideas, too. We should ask to use their photos to put some action into our brochure."

"Mr. Shaw promised to send some shots by e-mail, so I'll ask. Those finish line pileup photos might be misleading, though." His fingers strutted off her hand and onto her ribcage.

"Oh, you're not going to knock me down at every frolic and try to make me land on your bulk just to get some cheap public affection?" She plucked his trespassing fingers off and squinted at him as though to analyze his intent.

"Hey, that accident was not premeditated. I just overpowered your gait, that's all." His fingers alighted on the ball of her shoulder and she scrunched her neck. Next, he found the sweet scoop at the base of her neck and let his thumb troll through it. Her eyes flashed a response in contrast to shallow annoyance, so he nestled down against her side to fan the flames. "You know, you're kind of feisty when it's late and you're tired."

"And hurt," she added, blinking with intentional

slowness.

Her reddish-gold lashes did a number on his chest. Continuing their inspection, his fingers traced the line of her chin, sliding up toward her ear. Her loose hair felt like contraband silk as his hand fell away from his control. "I should make it all better."

Fallon looked at him, the softness in her eyes undeniable.

"But what could a lowly fisherman offer as a cure?" His breath swept her cheek where the shimmer of her porcelain skin shined between the freckled constellations.

In a heartbeat, her eyes glimmered to diamonds beneath the slaying lashes. "Guess he should make his best cast and see what happens." Her injured foot flexed against his.

He slid his toes beneath her arch to caress it as the distance between them closed to a promise-width. "They say casting's all in the wrist action." His upper lip grazed her mouth as he braced above her. With a heavenly handful of her hair, he wasn't about to demonstrate his point.

She nestled against him. "That's your last tip of the day, lock runner."

What started as a nibble turned into a full-fledged strike as he melted into a good catch and let a deeper emotion replace his tiredness. Not only did this bonus fish put up a little fuss, the exchange proved much more mutually sustainable. Not a bad day at the pond, he concurred, even if he was inland and duly landlocked.

~

Church the next morning turned into a blur of unfamiliar faces and lively praise songs. Court took them all in stride but had only one mission in mind. The tide had turned for him last night, and he wouldn't rest until he had pursued it with a gentleman's honor. After the service, he followed Warren out to the car while the women spoke with the pastor.

"Sir, if I could have a word with you…about Fallon." He paused as Warren looked up. "I, well, she means a lot to me, and I would like to have your permission to let her know I'm starting to feel serious about us."

Warren winked like he already knew. "I'll let you dig a bait fish pond out back, if it helps you re-situate any."

Court stopped short of the car, wondering if he'd gotten an answer to his courtship question. *Why does it always come down to fish?*

Chapter 18

Fallon shot a glance at the door, unprepared for the visit.

"These came off the fax machine and I thought you might need them," Sheri said, walking right into the office.

Fallon reached for the papers as her guest snapped to his feet, obviously interested in the source of their disruption. "Sheri Ware, this is Andy Lewis from the Port Mayaca lock. Andy, this is Liam's mother and my best friend, even when she disrupts my training class."

Sheri looked sheepish for an instant, but sobered under the man's gaze. She stuck a tentative hand out and he took it with generous attention, pumping it several times.

"Sheri runs the campground for us and does a fantastic job."

"You must be part saint dealing with the likes of those complainers," Andy replied, his grin breaking protocol.

Sheri pressed her lips together as though stunned at

the personal attention.

Fallon intervened for the rescue. "Maybe you could give Andy a tour of the campground during our lunch break later." She raised her eyebrows high enough to bring rain, hoping to leverage the woman out of her immediate stupor.

"That'd be sweet, but don't feel like you have to trouble yourself," Andy said.

"No trouble, no trouble at all." Sheri's frozen features relaxed into something quite charming as she held his gaze just long enough to drive her affirmative response home.

"We'll come over at the end of this session. Should we call?" Fallon tipped her head to gain the distracted woman's focus.

Sheri blinked and turned toward her, nodding and then thinking better of it. "Oh, just come over whenever. I'll be at the front desk unless someone's tent catches fire."

"Now I might have to pray for midday showers," Andy replied. His chin dropped, but not his gaze.

"Sorry for the interruption, Fallon. Good to meet you, Mr. Lewis." Sheri backed away and disappeared back down the stairs, her neck beet red.

Fallon walked the papers over to Charlie's desk and by the time she turned her attention back to her trainee, he had taken a sentinel position up by the front glass. She scanned the scene to determine what he found so interesting. Only the twin locks lay below with the grassy causeway in between.

"You've got a nice setup here," he said, wonderment lacing his voice. "Really nice."

"Thank you. Charlie Ware is unbelievably great to

work for, and the public stays captivated with the park. We're pretty busy. How about you guys?"

"Nope, we lack the amenities that you guys have. No park, no campground. It's plain nuts and bolts up there. We lift the boats, we lower the boats. No frills…and little appreciation."

"Guess working for the US Army Corps of Engineers isn't supposed to be glamorous. Otherwise, they wouldn't dress us in khaki blandness. We'd better get back to the workbook."

"You're right. The sooner we're done, the sooner we can break for lunch." Andy gave her a slight grin.

She caught the hint that he looked forward to the promised tour. Too bad she'd have to spend the next forty-five minutes searching for a legitimate reason to leave him alone with Sheri. This impromptu matchmaking thing could boomerang back on her in a hurry. If only she were better at ducking. At her insistence, the safety workbook fluttered open to the next section on potential hazards and the words sat pancake-flat on the page.

~

Court put down his frolic expense list and punched the calculator off as his brother banged through the backdoor.

"You are not going to believe this." Carter doubled over as boxes of bulk cookies spilled out of his arms.

Court rescued them to the counter. "Tell me and blow my mind. Then I'll be better suited to sit here all day." He took another case and placed them onto the counter, locking onto his brother's glowing face.

"Tessa's blood work came back. The problem is her thyroid—not her attitude."

"You mean, you're not driving her into depression?" He flashed a shocked look and pretended to flick a chip off his younger brother's shoulder.

"Guess I'm *not* guilty. Thanks, Court. And she's already on the medication to bring her levels back to normal. All she has to do is take a pill every day. Imagine that."

"She going to stay at her mother's awhile longer?" The question came with a personal barb, but Carter wouldn't hesitate to withhold information.

"Well, I haven't gotten that far, but I was planning to discuss it with her Friday. Maybe I'll ask her to come home for the weekend, since I can take care of the kids and let her rest."

"Try not to push her, Carter. Love finds the right way to bridge the gap."

"Listen to you, a sudden expert in the love department. Guess your weekend event was a big success?" Carter reached for his paperwork, grinning like a grouper.

He blocked the attempt with his forearm. "How should I describe it—organized chaos with lots of fish on the line? Saddle sore accountants had the gall to beat Fallon and me at the three-legged race. We had food galore with little left over. Plus, we received a bonus that has me wondering what to do with it. Truth be told, I had a blast and can hardly wait to do it all again. We've got four inquiry calls waiting to set the date. I'm thinking about launching a new venue at Lake Okeechobee next. I hope that sounds like getting the ball rolling, because that's what it feels like to me. Got any suggestions, Mr. Entrepreneur?"

Carter tore open the first box of snacks and started

restocking the shelves. "I'd say put the bonus money where you think you're thin. You borrowed rods, right? Then invest in your own equipment first. Save some of the bonus back to fund the next event so everything's not coming out of your pocket."

Court lent a hand and took the empty container, throwing it in the back. "We already cleared enough profit on the base fee to fund our next event, but I like your rod purchase idea. I should shop around and get some prices."

"Yeah, take off after lunch. No need for us both to be here at the shop."

"Carter, I want to figure out a way for the fishing frolics to pay back something into the shop. It could open up some opportunities for us beyond what Dad's been able to do. Think about it. Besides this innovative snack bar thing you've got going, what more could this place be if we bolstered our effort?"

"Maybe we could get some hired help on weekends, so I could enjoy my family more. Plus, it would free you up if you and Fallon got serious." He rocked on his heels, looking smart and impish at the same time.

"The thing is, if I get these fishing frolics scheduled on a regular basis, my weekends here are history. As for Fallon, I definitely need to find a way to keep her working with me on this. She transforms it from work to play and kicks me into higher gear somehow, even though I almost turned her into a cripple during the games segment."

"You're suave as usual, big brother, but I see some mellowing around the edges going on with you. Hey, don't tease me about my snack bar idea. Last week we sold the same amount of people food as fish food. You didn't think that would happen, did you?"

"Okay, you're the junior genius and I'm the conservative older brother. But from now on, it's not all work trying to keep this bait shop going. Invest in your family—and your dreams. Look at Callie Ann. She's going for her dream marrying Brian on Labor Day weekend."

"He's all right, even if he doesn't fish. He can still learn to be a good brother-in-law."

"Yeah, I'd better be his teacher because you didn't show too much skill at the bass tournament Memorial Day. Good thing we brought the kid with us."

"Give me grief, but at least I still have my winnings in the bank, which is more than you can say. Maybe I'll take Tessa and the kids to the mountains this fall. Hey, remember to keep your eye out for real estate. Brian and Callie can't find a house in their price range. At this rate, they won't even be able to close before the wedding."

"No promises there, as I'm swamped trying to get this fishing frolic to gain traction. I need to get on these call-backs and set some dates for more bookings. Can you work quietly for a change?" He reached for the shop phone and Carter stepped back into the storage room, his hands showing full surrender. A customer stepped in the front door and the dream session had to wait for one more bait sale. Carter emerged, motioning for him to stay put, and addressed the man's order. Court gave the man a nod, sent a prayer up for success, and dialed the first number. He would cast his bread upon the corporate waters to see if he could get another nibble.

~

Fallon noted that Sheri had neatened her appearance and now wore a bit of eye makeup which lightened her dark features. Andy followed her into the campground office and pulled off his cap as he nodded to their tour host. Sheri closed the book she'd been reading and stood behind the counter, wiping the wrinkles from her capris.

"Here we are, as promised," Fallon said. She attempted to add several cheery notes to her announcement even though she really wanted to bolt back out the door.

Sheri lifted a hand and motioned toward the rear room. "Let's start here where all the real work is done," she replied. Andy stepped toward the doorway and nodded sideways for her to go first. A little smile followed, making it impossible for Sheri to decline.

Fallon suppressed a smile and slung her lunch cooler on the front counter. She glimpsed the phone on the desk and thought of an easy out. "Maybe I should spell you at the front desk in case the phone rings."

"No need. I have an answering machine and will get back to them when I can. We're full now anyway, so nothing's that urgent. Come with us." They disappeared into the back room.

Fallon forced herself to follow. The hum of a dryer met her on the other side.

"We have twelve tent sites along the canal and twelve RV sites on the landward side. In addition to each campsite, which has a picnic table and grill, we try to provide ancillary services such as refrigeration, an ice machine, and a laundry facility. We figured all this out as we went along since our campers tend to be long-term, with fewer weekend stays." Sheri walked across the room as Andy studied every detail.

Fallon tried to mentally teleport out of the room to somewhere more scenic. The smell of dryer sheets brought her right back.

"Sheri, take a look at this outlet a second," Andy said, kneeling by the folding table.

In seconds Sheri had shimmied down next to him and regarded the outlet as though it held some fascinating interest.

He touched the splitter and pulled back like it smarted. "It's red hot, just like I thought. You're overloaded here. It's a potential electrical hazard for sure. If I were you, I'd run that mini refrigerator off another outlet, like that one under the table there, to spread out your load."

Sheri dared a direct look and worked through his suggestion as if it contained some degree of higher thought. "I totally agree. Could you go ahead and switch it before I blow a fuse? I could find you some gloves or something."

"No need. I'll get it." Before the dryer could take another spin, he'd reached into his pocket for a tissue, folded it around the plug, and made the transfer to the unused outlet. Rising too soon under the table, his head came up destined for a bang, but Sheri put out a protective hand and capped his curly crown just in time.

"Good teamwork, you two," Fallon said, making light of the personal encounter.

Andy righted in a full blush, his eyes fixed on Sheri.

Fallon had to look away and when her cell phone vibrated, she almost let a hallelujah slip out. "It's Court. I really should get this Sheri. I hope you don't mind."

Andy stood stock still. "If Bait Crate needs some

help, tell him I can pitch in."

"Thanks Andy. That's kind of you to offer. I'll be sure to tell him." Retrieving the call, she exited the campground building as fast as her feet could manage with any dignity, abandoning the third wheel position with due haste."Hey Court. Great timing, I'm at lunch. What's up?"

"How's the ankle today? Have I left you a lonesome cripple?"

"Oh, I wish. Then I wouldn't have gotten hoodwinked into touring the campground with Andy Lewis. He's in for safety training today."

"Good old Andy from Port Mayaca locks. How's he getting along?"

"Well, believe it or not, I think he's on a magnetic conveyor belt headed straight for our favorite campground manager." She tried to hold back the girlish snicker but failed, and Court leveraged it up to a full laugh in response. "I acted like this call might need special attention just to get me out of the tour loop. Shame on me, right? I hope you're not in emergency mode."

"No, but I always need special attention when it comes to you. I'm really out shopping for fishing poles. Carter and I discussed re-investing the bonus. I'd like to have our own gear instead of loaners. What do you think about junior-sized poles? I'm standing in front of a rack of super hero poles that are on clearance. I could get half a dozen for the smaller kids."

"Describe them to me, I mean the working parts, like the reel."

"It's open, which I prefer. They're all black resin with decals from the handles up the rod, for maybe an eyelet or two. I see Spiderman, Superman, and the green guy."

She heard him testing a reel. "That's the Incredible Hulk. Well, if you like the poles, get two of each character for now. We can make a special rack for them if they're too short."

"Wow. I hadn't even thought of storage. No wonder I called you. That gives Warren another project with me. He might get tired of that."

"Are you kidding? He's probably making a list of improvements back at the rental shop right now. He's as on fire for this as you are, Court." She slid onto the top of a picnic table under the front porch overhang, facing into the breeze.

"I sure don't deserve all this help, but it certainly is welcome. Okay, I'm grabbing six of these babies and heading out to the next store to compare prices on the big boy stuff."

"Wait a minute. Aren't you forgetting my consulting fee?"

"That's going to be hard to pay over the phone."

She enjoyed the buzz his tone prompted. "Sometimes you only need to pay attention."

"Oh, I can sure do that. These super heroes can wait a few. I'll stand here and keep my eyes on them and my ears on you. How does that sound?"

"My morning's been a boring mix of protocol and safety savvy. How about you? What's going on at the shop?"

"Carter came in with an armload of snack supplies. He claims that the people food is selling as good as the fish food."

"Kudos to Carter then, for seizing the opportunity

and all."

"And get this. Tessa's blood work came back with a thyroid deficiency. She has to take some synthetic supplement every day, but it's totally curable. You were right after all."

"Keep talking like that. You're making my day. What else?"

"He wants her back home, of course, but I told him not to force it."

"Good advice. She'll come back on her terms at first, and then they can work on it."

"And Callie must be getting antsy about not being able to find a house. Carter doesn't think they can close on anything by the wedding. By the way, you plan to attend, don't you? I want you there with us, more specifically with me. I don't want to look like a total loser having both my baby sister and my little brother beat me down the aisle."

"I would love to attend and be seen with the bride's distinguished older brother. And remember, the last time you tried to rush down a lane it didn't end up very pretty, did it?"

"Ouch. Guess I deserved that. Now, I really am wishing you were right here with me so I could see that devilish look in your eyes while you play victim to my two left feet."

"I think it's biblical to interject that one reaps what one sows, Mr. Reynolds."

"Hold that thought, Miss McKenzie, because I fully intend to. But for right now, I'd better give these half-priced gentlemen my full attention and let you get your lunch eaten."

"Have fun shopping without me."

"We'll get together soon, I promise. After all, I scheduled three more frolics this morning, so it looks like we're destined for more side by side fun."

"That's fantastic, Court. Congrats, you've got this thing moving forward."

"You make everything special," he said in a lower tone. "Think about July fourth and let's make some private plans."

"Will do. I'll look forward to it. Are you coming over my way anytime this week? I'd hate to let Liam get all of your attention."

"Tell you what. Pack a double lunch tomorrow and Friday. I'll hang around and keep you from getting too lonesome once I get his bait fish loaded."

"I'm that transparent, aren't I?"

"I miss being out there. Tell Andy Lewis that I'm jealous."

"Okay. He said to tell you he could help Bait Crate with anything, just give him the word." She put her hand to her throat to help massage out the lump that started to form.

"Let's take a rain check on his offer, as something always comes up, especially with a teenager in a boat on Lake O. Stay off that hurt foot. I don't want a limping leading lady for my next event. You have two weeks. We're doing a retirement party next."

"Oh, goodie. An older clientele. Maybe I won't have to run at all."

"Don't count on it. See you tomorrow around eleven."

"Good-bye, Court. Enjoy your super heroes." The phone clicked to silence and she pocketed it, gazing out at the lock across the parking lot. Andy was right. They had a nice setup, but without the Bait Crate boat coming through, it seemed high and dry to her.

~

"I stopped myself at twelve rods, but I can always add on more," Court said, fingering the filling of his deviled egg. "That lets me keep some of the bonus in case I want to get crazy with it over the summer." He gave Fallon a crafty look.

"Taking on a new business already makes you certifiable." She turned sideways to better see the canal from their shady spot in the campground. "Tell me more about this retirement gig."

"Some close friends are going to steal this guy away and not tell him anything. They're leaving it to me where they'll end up. I'm planning for fifteen men who want fishing and food."

"Are you ready to try Lake Okeechobee? That seems like a reasonable group size to pull something off on the city dock. You could handle the food tailgate-style right out of the truck."

"Wow, that sounds so doable. Would you help me, Fallon? Once I get the hang of it, I might solo, but not from the start."

"I don't want you to solo. Then where would I be on a lonesome weekend? Left back at the cabin where the party isn't?" She made a baby carrot disappear into her mouth.

"Okay, it's set. You're with me for the retirement frolic. We should walk the site before then and think through the setup. In the meantime, I'll inquire about reserving the dock with a call to town hall."

"I looked at celebrations for the Fourth of July and the biggest show around happens to be over Lake O.

They're having a military band at the amphitheater right before dark, and then fireworks over the lake. I thought it might be memorable." She turned back toward him only to divert her gaze toward the campground office.

When a screen door slammed closed, he turned to give the intruder the evil eye.

Sheri came toward them with her hands folded behind her back. "Excuse the breech of privacy, but I come in peace." She produced an American flag mounted on a pencil. "Andy Lewis is on the phone. He wants to know if you two could join us for the Independence Day celebration at the lake Saturday night."

"Hey, we were just talking about that. It's up to you, Fallon. Want to?"

"Sheri, are you good with this? I'd hate to crash your first date."

"Crash away. It might make me more comfortable with you guys there, anyway. Then if it doesn't work out too great, I have a backup ride home."

"Court has another fishing frolic scheduled and we're thinking about checking out the city dock to see how accommodating it would be as the event site. I hope that wouldn't seem too much like mixing business with pleasure." She ate another baby carrot while Sheri processed the idea.

"We'll all end up at the water's edge anyway, right? That's the best place to see the fireworks reflect off the lake. I think they shoot them off a barge, don't they?"

"Ask Andy. I've always been on the river up in Stuart for the fireworks show," he admitted. "Guess this will be my first time trapped inland."

"Tell him we'd be happy to make it a foursome,

Sheri," Fallon replied. "I'll work on Court's attitude so he doesn't feel so *trapped*." She squinted at him while Sheri handed her the flag and jogged back to the building.

"In my defense, I'm from the coast where life is open-ended, at least to the east." He captured the hand holding the flag and thought he'd regained ground rather well.

"Don't close us landlocked folks out, coastal guy," Fallon replied with a warning tone.

When she started to bite into another innocent baby carrot, he decided right then and there the slaughter had to end. From her surprise, he must not have moved like a trapped man. Lunch soon gained a delicious ending that had nothing whatsoever to do with nutrition.

Chapter 19

The conductor dragged out the final strains of Battle Hymn of the Republic and the red-cheeked band members obliged. The song ended in a bit of disharmony, but still generated ample applause. Fallon slapped the back of her calf wishing for the bug spray in her glove box.

Sheri stepped away from the crowd following Andy. "We'd better go stake out our place on the dock."

"Hey, Fallon. Want me to get that bug spray?" Court pointed toward the parking lot. When she handed him the keys, he jogged away on a mission for the greater good.

She caught up with Sheri as their secret mantra came back to her. "Life to the full," she whispered as they crossed the street.

"I'm really excited," Sheri replied. "He's so nice."

As if on cue, Andy turned around from the curbside and reached for her hand.

Sheri fluttered her eyelashes back in girl code.

Fallon received the message loud and clear. To keep

from being the third party again, she headed for the far side of the dock, determined to step it off and give Court a distance estimate. Since he couldn't reserve the facility for a private party, at least they could maximize their options for sharing it. She'd paced off ten steps when a heavy hand halted her progress.

There stood Kit Rawlings, off duty and drunk as a coon on fermented pokeberry. "What's this lovely little firefly that's come to shine tonight?" He tugged her toward him.

She pried his fingers off her arm and thrust his hand clear. "We've been over this before, Rawlings. I'll thank you not to touch me ever again." She took a bold step toward her friends and felt something snag her shirttail. A shudder raced up her back while she tried not to panic.

As she twisted to escape his grasp, a fist flew past her shoulder and landed squarely on the drunk's jaw. He hit the dock hard as the rescuer's hand scooped hers and pulled her into a run. Andy eased the abrupt departure with a conspirator's wink and brought her to Sheri, who buried her shocked expression in her palms.

She took a second to smooth her outfit and let out a breath. "Please don't let this ruin the night for Court," she said, looking between Sheri and Andy.

Court leapt onto the dock and began to pump bug spray onto the back of her legs. "You're shaking all over. The bugs must really be after you." He held out her arm to spray it.

"See what happens when you leave?" Sheri asked, taking Andy's hand in hers. "That girl just falls to pieces. Stick tight from now on, will you Court?" She gave Andy a coy tilt of her head and he moved closer.

"This feels better. Thanks so much. Sheri, want some spray? The mosquitoes are awful."

"I'll wait for the first bite before I apply DEET to my skin. Andy, how about you?"

"I'm immune," he said with a laugh. "Years of working outside have left me with leathery skin. Those skeeters couldn't punch through my hide if they had to."

"Where were you before the locks? Guess I never thought to ask before," Court said.

"San Diego. I'm retired US Coast Guard. I took a random stab at opportunity and chose Florida for my encore career. Here I am, thirty-seven years old and starting all over again. I'm all about boats, which has me wondering why in the world I bought a little farmhouse in Indiantown. Convenient, I guess. It's close to work."

Sheri fanned her face. "I'm thirsty. Can I get anyone a drink from the stand over there?"

Fallon started to reply, but quickly realized her friend meant to target someone else.

"Let me take you over," Andy insisted. "Rough-looking crowd out tonight."

"You could tell me about that little farmhouse while we walk," Sheri replied, looking keenly interested.

Court wrapped his arm around Fallon's waist. "Bring us one to share, will you?"

Andy gave a mock salute and gestured for Sheri to lead.

"Indiantown isn't far from here, is it?" Sheri asked, matching her gait with Andy's.

A wave of guilt came over Fallon. She could level with Court now without any additional fallout, but she wanted to redeem the night more than anything.

"You seem to be settling down. What got into you back there?"

"Oh, I decided to step off the length of the dock for you, but a drunk bumped into me and got me all flustered. Andy knocked his lights out and brought me back to Sheri, which is when you came back with the spray."

His brow knit as he searched her face. "Well? How long is the dock, little miss business-before-pleasure?" He touched her nose with a finger.

She buried her face in his chest. "I lost count, what an idiot." She inhaled and enjoyed the clean cotton smell of his polo shirt, letting it appease her raw nerves.

He lifted her chin and wove his gaze into hers. "Repeat after me. No more business. Only pleasure." His thumbs stroked her cheek to coax out the confession.

"I am standing here on the edge of my favorite lake with the most incredible man I've ever met. No more business. Only pleasure. I promise." Her last words were tamped down by the arrival of his lips. It was a quick peck, since they were in a public place, but it came right when she needed it most.

~

Fireworks exploded like meteors on entry, setting the atmosphere over the lake in carnival colors. A night heron squawked down below the dock and Court tried to make out its hasty flight departing the area under siege. Fallon backed into him as the first boom split the air and he held her there under his chin, covering her arms from the bug brigade breeding in the shallows. Glittery extensions arched out from the sky explosion and traipsed down to the water's surface which reflected them back up again. The effect mesmerized him. He heard Fallon gasp in pleasure. The next shell went up and gold dust showered the sky in all directions.

"I liked that one," Sheri said.

"Try squinting as they cascade down," Andy replied, moving closer to her.

Court squeezed his eyes nearly closed and the points of light blurred to liquid. Fallon made a throaty noise of approval which he felt more than heard. He kissed her hair. Three cannons went off next. Red, white, and blue explosions streaked the sky. He could smell gunpowder now as a light breeze played off the water. At this rate, they would smoke the mosquitoes out and take back the night by the end of the show. Of course, the fishing might be puny tomorrow morning, but that wasn't his problem tonight.

An array of rapid-fire silver spiders lit the sky followed by a wake of reflection from the water. Caught off-guard, the crowd murmured over the display and Sheri clapped like a little girl. Andy bent and whispered something to her, making her nod her head in agreement.

Fallon looked up at him and a red ball exploded midair, reflecting in her eyes. Screamers corkscrewed out from the center, so she plugged her ears and smiled. "Hope your expression isn't one of a trapped man."

He hugged her against his chest. "I'm fallen—but not trapped." He sealed his declaration on the rim of her ear. When she shuddered in his arms, it quaked right through him.

~

"Are you seeing that man from the bait shop?" the star of the retirement party asked, walking Fallon back to the dock after a rousing round robin of checkers under the water oaks.

"Yes, sir. I work at the St. Lucie locks and Court came through one day at the same time a recreational boater had a heart attack. He kept him alive until we got the lock open so the EMTs could get to him. His heroism really caught my attention."

"Fishing is the perfect portal to the inside of a man," he said. "It shows patience."

"And you have to take a read below the surface where the striking action is. Anyway, I think we've been good for each other. He's drawing me out from being a loner."

"Now, that would have been a waste." He smiled and shifted to the left side of the dock, taking his pick of the poles Court had leaning against the rail. "What about your influence on him?" His bushy brow rose like a question mark.

She split her attention between his gray eyes and the lake. "Well, I would answer by saying that sometimes life hurts, and being a connector has an immediate backlash to it. I've been a safe haven for him whenever ill winds blow."

"Aha, that's the comfort of the leeward side. I've needed to visit there myself a time or two and it's quite restorative." He rubbed across his upper lip.

"I live inland so, at first, I felt like I might be a misplaced distraction. His family is entrenched on the coast, being in the bait business and all."

"He treats you like a distraction, does he?" He tested a blue fiberglass rod by pulling on the line, watching the tip flex under duress.

"No, he treats me like…a blessing."

"Two minutes until the fishing competition begins," Court called, rolling up the cooler."Maybe you should seize the moment, then," the old man suggested, handing her the pole. His bushy brow arched as he stopped Court and motioned for some of the bait he carried. "You can thank me later," he added, shooting the unsuspecting host a wizened glance.

Fallon watched his longtime buddies walk onto the dock, shoulders locked and ready for bragging rights as his reel zinged with the first lucky cast. Court could end this on a high note if the fish would cooperate. Maybe the slippery critters had forgotten all about the fireworks antics and had grown hungry for bloodworms by now. A quick strike ended with a bass over the rail in record time. She had her takeaway, plus a word-to-the-wise nugget tucked in her back pocket.

~

The night grew late as his headlights swiped across familiar cinderblock houses up Centerboard Lane. Court leaned over the wheel as thoughts of Fallon serving chocolate raspberry cake to his happy fishermen flitted through his head. He slowed for the drive and checked the back of the bait shop before he turned in. A solitary beam of light panned across the back ponds. His ease extinguished like a snuffed candle when a shadow moved. Almost midnight, nothing should be going on down there. A pinprick of concern made his chest wince. He hoped Carter remembered to lock up.

He shoved in the headlight knob and crept down the street with only his parking lights and two street lights contributing any illumination. The moon would be late rising, which all too frequently contributed to the delinquency of a minor who had petty theft on the brain. Not in the mood for mischief, he fought the urge to reverse the truck and go straight to bed. A light beam dashed across the building and went out. Someone was clearly up to no good.

He pulled his phone out of his chest pocket and slid it into his cargo shorts. The truck halted on the roadside off the back pond. The light flashed on and off again. He eased out of the cab, drawing on residual strength.

In steps, he'd made the backyard. Someone sat hunched against the door and moaned when he made contact. A flashlight came at him and he grabbed it on reflex, punching it on to illuminate the culprit. Blood dripped down a slashed wrist which he found attached to a teary-faced teenager bent on self-destruction. "Tanner?"

He crouched beside the waif who barely acknowledged his presence. When the boy reached out to him, he saw with nightmarish clarity that the other wrist already ebbed with the same red tide. His reaction to the sight of blood came too fast to control. He turned and gave in, losing his dinner beside the back steps.

He knelt to stabilize. "Hold on, buddy. We're gonna get you out of this." He focused, dialing in the emergency. The line picked up right away as he keyed the back lock to gain entry to the shop. "Ambulance," he replied, searching for the pile of clean rags they kept by the mop closet. He took the top one and started back out the door. "I found a teenager on the back steps of my business and his wrists are slit. I have a clean towel. Tell me what to do." A voice murmured back confirming his location and narrated a treatment to remedy the bleeding. He ripped the rag in half, kneeling in front of the boy. With the flashlight balanced on the middle step, he applied pressure to the left wound.

Tanner dropped his chin, his face drained. "Life hurts too much without Audie here."

"She'd want us to find our courage in times like this. I need you to be strong. Can you do that for me?" He cuffed the second towel strip around the right wrist and tucked the tail under to hold fast. Blood dripped everywhere, His hands became slick from the contact.

An organic smell made his stomach heave, but nothing came up his throat. Lights soon flickered across the bait pond and the help he needed arrived on four wheels. Head spinning, he elevated the injured limbs on his shoulders and waited for the rescuers. Only then did it strike him to pray, his faith now proving every bit as feeble as his fortitude. "Lord, fix what's broken here and stop the loss before anyone else goes down, I beg you. Take Tanner and make him whole again, inside and out, amen."

Within minutes, two men rushed up to them with a gurney. The taller man touched the teen's neck as his assistant moved into place. Seconds later, the team had the boy loaded and headed for the ambulance double doors. He followed in mechanical motion, gaining ground and being left behind all at the same time.

"We're inbound for Martin Memorial. Think you can notify the boy's parents?"

He gestured to the EMTs as the vehicle departed, throwing sand with the rear wheels. Hobbling back to the steps for his phone, he caught sight of the blood drying on his hands. He returned to the first bait pond and knelt to rinse clean. A shiner darted from the surface, wary of the late-night intrusion. With blood up to his elbows, he even scared himself. When he stood, the moon broke the horizon over Manatee Pocket as if to peek at the action.

"You're too late," he said with flat indignation. His foot kicked the flashlight as he stepped up to lock the back door. The resulting spin of light carved by its beam described the churning he felt inside. *How can I live like this?* The key turned in the lock and he jogged back to his truck. Now he had to go ruin the evening for Tanner's parents. The antithesis of connecting choked him as he cranked the ignition. Nausea returned with a vengeance, but he managed to get the truck window rolled down in time.

Chapter 20

The Egyptian sheets caressed her limbs with coolness, but she blamed the chocolate raspberry cake for her wakeful state. The blue display on her clock radio flipped to one o'clock. She was a hundred percent sure she couldn't sleep. Fallon sat up and propped her elbows on her knees, settling her chin into the cusp of her hands. Even rubbing her eyes didn't help.

The retirement party came to mind. She sifted through the old man's words of advice, trying to be sure she got the gist of his meaning. He'd told her to "seize the moment" which should have made sense, but it didn't seem to carry any traction in their date-around-work existence. Her phone vibrated against the glass-topped nightstand and she saw Court's number.

"Hey, what gives? Are you okay?" She heard labored breathing and tucked her hair back, pressing the phone closer to her ear. Seconds ticked by as she strained for any response. Her breath grew shallow. Her thoughts skated over ice-thin possibilities.

"I pulled onto Centerboard Lane just in time to find Tanner on the back steps at Bait Crate," he replied. Labored breathing filled the receiver.

She heard his struggle before she even knew the nature of it. "Okay. That was late for a fourteen-year-old to be out, midnight or so." She tried to inject a soothing balm into her tone, but hated to chatter on without due cause. A throaty sound came over the phone line and she braced for the explanation.

"Tanner slit his wrists over losing Audie."

The truth barreled down the hollow alley of comprehension, rocking her back onto her pillows. "Dear Lord, help us," she whispered. "Were you in time?"

"Yeah, the crazy thing is, I actually saw him make the second cut, as the light jerked when he did it. That's what caught my attention right before I turned in the driveway."

"Bless your heart, Court. You've saved that boy and spared his parents an unimaginable heartache." The line fell silent again and she heard footsteps on a hard surface. "Are you at the hospital with them now?"

"Yeah, the doctor promised to let us know something here in the next ten minutes or so. Tanner's asking for me, but his parents need to see him first. I can wait. He's going to want to talk about losing Audie. That's still a tough topic for me."

When she heard him struggle to swallow, the pain of separation became too much to bear. "I'm driving up there. Are you at Martin Memorial?"

"Yeah. ER waiting room. They'll be admitting him once he's been treated down here, but I'll wait for you."

She slid off the bed and grabbed her capris off the

hamper nearby. "Can I bring anything?"

"Listen, my shirt reeks with my typical reaction to blood. I lost it a couple of times."

"I have the extra Bait Crate shirts here. I'll bring you one. See you in thirty minutes."

"I sure need some help, but I don't deserve it, Fallon."

"My heart hurts when yours hurts, Court. I'm seizing the moment here. I have to."

"Call your parents before you leave. I don't want that on my record." His tone lightened an ounce.

She took it as a positive sign."I'll call as I'm driving out. See you soon." She ended the call and made a frantic dash into her closet to get dressed and find shoes. Seizing the moment had a mad rush to it, but it beat languishing in the background by fifty yards or more. The old fisherman's wise eyes flashed to mind and she strategized her heart's next move as her feet maneuvered toward the car.

~

A dull ache circled around the back of his head like he'd been whacked with an oar. Court slumped forward in the chair, having lost track of how long Tanner's parents had been in the curtained area. The emergency room pulsed with the next arrival as a baby being smothered by an oxygen mask rolled by strapped on a gurney. He tried not to look, too close to the edge of tolerance by his own circumstances. His life seemed like a dance routine gone bad, with one step forward and two steps back. The neighborhood crumbled, one neglected, misled kid at a time. How could he go back there, wash off the blood, and pretend everything was the same?

He blocked the light out of his eyes with cupped hands and let the buzz of tiredness take over. At least he didn't have to think anymore once he fell into the zone between awareness and blackout. When he came to, someone knelt beside him planting kisses in his hair.

His eyes eased open far enough to see that Fallon had arrived. He shifted his weight onto her frame and surrendered to the ache. The rain smell from her hair caught his tears and turned them into perfume, somehow diluting the putrid smell he'd brought with him. When her fingers combed through his hair, the dull headache dissipated into thin air.

"I'm here for you," she whispered, rocking him against her shoulder.

"I'm losing my grip," he replied. His ribcage soon quaked to prove it.

"Let God hold it together, Court. He's all-powerful. You've done enough for one day."

"First burnt candles on the curb and now blood all over the steps. It's too much to take."

"Hush. Don't think about it. Lord, in the name of Jesus and the power of the Holy Spirit, we release all these pain-filled hurts to you. We've done all mortals can do, dear God. Please step in and do the rest in your might, not our weakness, amen."

A shudder quaked through him, but she held him all the tighter. Limp in her arms, he hung on, broken and numb. "So hard to go back, clean up the mess, and act like it doesn't matter."

"Of course it matters, but you're not going back. I'm taking you to Loxahatchee."

He flinched in objection, but she held her ground. "Warren already knows and your room is waiting. No arguments.”

Weak and wounded, all he could do was nod and wipe his eyes in her hair. Her touch became satin to his raw-edged nerves, a soft place to land. When she began to hum the notes of a reverent praise song, he found the will to climb out of desperation's pit.

~

Fallon leaned out the open window and soaked in the healing morning air as her father drove down a country lane. Trees pressed the edge of the road, their canopies arching over to shade the entire width. The car slowed and angled into an opening in the trees, nosing into a dirt lot where fewer than twenty cars snuggled against a quaint old clapboard building.

"Where are we?" Court asked, his voice void of inflection due to their late night at the hospital. "Is this a church?"

"Cowboy church," Janine replied, turning to the back seat with a smile. "We decided to keep it simple today."

"You might like this, the worship is heartfelt," Fallon assured him. She reached for him and his hand met hers halfway.

He ducked to see the spire's length. "This looks old Florida cracker-style, like something my granddaddy could have attended."

"Only this particular building got purchased from the Pentecostals," Warren said. "It's a wonder the floor joists haven't given out." Her mother popped a corrective hand on his shoulder and the men exchanged glances in the rearview mirror. Fallon rolled her window to within an inch of the top seal and opened her door as soon as the engine turned off.

The little white church with pink oleander bushes

skirting its foundation greeted them with the grace of God. Court met her where the broken sidewalk began and they walked up together. She took the first step as he laid a pink blossom on her Bible. She anchored it there with her thumb. Her smile found a man searching for peace, looking right in her direction.

"Should I have worn my cowboy hat?" He pointed to a branding logo around the name placard at the front door. He pulled the brass latch and her mom and dad stepped inside.

"Probably, but at least they take them off for prayer." She hooked him with her smile and brought him into a place where a weary soul could find rest. The simple gesture brought her an intense satisfaction. She was good for him.

~

With the opening scriptures read by a man in jeans wearing cowboy boots, Court could tell the service wouldn't wear the pretentious tone of organ pipes and lumpy sopranos hiding under choir robes. A thin man with a drooping moustache took a seat on a bar stool and began to strum his guitar. The folks on the front row stood, so the rest followed. He sang a familiar praise song about blessings and curses being on the same road to God. To keep the man's twitching moustache from distracting him, Court locked his gaze on the peeled-bark cross over the altar.

The second verse held a line about "pain in the offering" and it came to him that his recent rough stretch might have been a test of spiritual endurance. He pressed his calves on the pew's seat and closed his eyes, reflecting on Audie's constant hunger for attention and Tanner's vulnerability. Carter's imbalance over Tessa's estrangement came to mind next, followed by Callie's plans to be wed to Brian with nowhere decent to live.

Life's complexity soon got the best of him and his trunk started to sway as dizziness overtook him. Fallon's arm found his shoulders and eased him to the pew, her hip sliding against his for full support. Relieved that the singing ended in prayer, he buried his face in his hands and called out in silence to God. No tears came with the plea. He had no tears left.

The next speaker didn't appear to be on the roster, but he stepped up with such surety that the leader wearing a pearl button shirt nodded his immediate consent. Unfolding a piece of notebook paper from his breast pocket, he cleared his throat and began to read.

"My trail ends at the Crystal Lake," he said, hesitating from the introduction to get duly situated.

The paper shook a bit and Court could readily relate, which purchased some ease.

"Whatever turns this life might take, however far from kin and home,

Nor setbacks from wrong turns I make that could cause my pony to roam;

Lord, lead me on for progress' sake far away from the billow's foam,

Guide me past the tempter's mistake to the blest shore where angels come;

My trail ends at the Crystal Lake, where I'll make my eternal home."

Eyes closed and chin tucked against his chest, foaming waves broke across Court's minds-eye as he wrestled with his lifelong attachment to the coast. Lake Okeechobee beckoned like the idyllic Crystal Lake of the cowboy's destination. Between lay all the painful jabs of the tempter's mistakes. He'd taken a few of those in the ribs lately, proving his adeptness at learning a lesson might be somewhat hindered. Maybe the time had come for him to ask the Lord to lead him on up the trail toward the angels. He opened his eyes and Fallon filled his field of vision.

"I think we might have already had a little sermon thrown at us this morning," the preacher quipped. "Thank you, Sonny, for putting it so clearly. We're destined for heaven as believers, so we might let it temper our trail drive along the way. Now turn with me to Matthew, chapter five. This passage on The Beatitudes will be as familiar as the back forty to most of you, but gaze deeper into God's word as I reflect today on why ordinary people need to be blessed."

Court sat erect, knowing he would take this message right between the eyes. The lyrical rhythm of the paired verses spoke to his heart as the man read them without any hurry. A hunger to find truth within the passage began to gnaw at him even though the translation being shared differed from the one Fallon's fingertip traced. Restless, he finally pinpointed his difficulty as the closing lines spoke of persecuted prophets. He leaned close until his chin touched her shoulder. "Do you love me enough to write this for me in… lake language?" he whispered.

"I do, and I will," she replied, her silky cheek brushing his. She closed the Bible as the preacher called for prayer to bless the reading of God's Word.

Here he sat, a man torn between shore and lake, but realized even the poor in spirit gained entitlement to the kingdom of God. He let go a little bit as the sermon began, allowing the sea breeze to blow him inland toward these God-fearing folks. Warren leaned forward and looked at him, passing along a fatherly nod as though everything would work out in the end.

~

Fallon fanned her face in the shade behind the campground office to offset July's oppressive heat. With Sheri delayed, Court's call had come halfway through a tuna sandwich. Their first attempt at a fishing frolic at Sandsprit Park the previous Saturday bore the ragged edge of a terrier's favorite slipper. Troubleshooting pushed against the day's heat as Court held that more ice would have been the solution.

"Go ahead and get another big cooler." She pressed her icy water bottle against her neck.

"Why not, right? I have room in the back of the truck. Plus, I think I'd like to go ahead and buy more rods with the money we cleared."

"That sounds reasonable. Water traffic is dead here today. Charlie has me catching up paperwork for district office. I'm telling you what, the heat is brutal."

"Yeah, the bait shop is in meltdown, too. Carter found out he couldn't buy anything chocolate and keep the frosting on it."

Sheri appeared outside the door a millisecond, and then went back inside. She heard a knock and glanced around, then finally realized it came over the phone.

Court growled. "Hold on a second. Deidra's at my back door."

She switched her phone to speaker and picked up her sandwich before it spoiled. Sheri came out with a misting spray bottle that had a tiny battery-operated fan in front. When she aimed it at her face, it brought cooling relief.

Court's voice amped up in the background as the not-so-neighborly conversation ignited. "Pay more attention to your children, how about it?"

Sheri nodded to the phone. "Court?"

"Sounds like he's at odds with his next-door neighbor."

"The little girl left at the beach? That family?"

Fallon nodded and tried to swallow. Unease made her skin creep.

Court's tone grew adamant. A door slammed shut. "What? *You* for a girlfriend? Believe me, the last thing I need is a girlfriend."

Feeling the immediate sting, Fallon punched the phone to kill the call, trying not to react.

"What just happened? Did their conversation detonate?"

"You might be right," Fallon replied, choking back something more unsavory than her stale lunch. "I'm going for a walk to try and forget he said that."

"You know he didn't mean *you*." Sheri brushed her arm with a flip of her wrist.

Fallon made quick work of leaving the scene of trespass, her phone still weighing down the table. Court might dial her back, but she didn't want to talk—not to a man so adamant about not needing a girlfriend. The heart poke proved too direct, even from an eavesdropper's distance.

Chapter 21

Court hadn't seen Fallon for two weeks. Every time he called, she always had a valid reason to prolong the streak. Fortunately, August had lessened its heat today so he planned a surprise visit to the locks. Making quick work of the lower canal, he gave his bait ballast the ride of its life. Unless Fallon could be wooed out of work to ride along, he would talk Liam into making the lake run in his boat. It seemed out of character for her to brood. They needed to talk.

The canal run straightened and he could see the bottom locks were already sealed shut, meaning he'd have to wait below. He'd pull up and make it obvious to the tower he required their service. If he hoisted a white flag, Fallon might even be willing to make an appearance along the flank. A man could only hope.

When a figure soon appeared in a gimpy run, apprehension needled under his sternum. At sixty-five years old, Charlie Ware didn't run for just any reason. His veins icing, he pulled the boat over to the west bank and cut the motor.

The chief tender knelt down on the concrete. "Court, we've got trouble on the nature trail. Liam spotted Rawlings' empty boat tied up north along the causeway. Fallon's trimming the boardwalk back there today since it's so mild. I've got the upper gate open, so nobody can access the east bank. I don't have a good feeling about this. She's put that uncouth game warden on report four times already. At least she's wearing her gun."

"I'll go over. Tell me how to gain access from down here." He tried not to let it sting that he didn't know this problem still existed. It chafed against the way she'd been holding him off.

"Use the maintenance stairs built into the second lock. Tie onto the cleat there and shimmy up the hand-holds. Be quick about it, as I can't say how long that boat's been there. I've had my hands full in the lock without her, but Liam's helping me now." The aging man stood and stiff-legged it back to the tower.

He fired the motor and made the boat cut to the east bank. His ability to reason floated out with the spillway's churning waters. Fallon needed protection. That's all that mattered. Talking it out could wait. A man on a mission, he needed to rendezvous with the trail crew chief and yank the fisheries agent out by the scruff of his red neck. He wrapped the bow line and wedged his foot into the carved-out foothold. Taking them two at a time, he soon crested the grassy surface of the causeway. With the trailhead in sight, his throat clamped shut.

~

"Don't do this," Fallon warned. No longer having the element of surprise, she resorted to reasoning with a lurid madman.

Rawlings laughed at her vulnerability as he hauled her field vest onto the boardwalk, glaring down at her where she stood in the wetland.

Now she had no gun, no radio, no phone, and little energy left. Midday cracked over her bare head since she'd tossed her hat under the boardwalk to leave a clue as to her whereabouts.

"I told you we'd finish this and it looks like today's your lucky day. We can proceed nice and friendly or I'll have to resort to…other tactics." He grinned, but it didn't last.

"I'm not going to comply with your inane fantasy. If you violate my personal space, I'll give you the fight of your life." She stepped upland to gain an advantage, thinking to make a run for the causeway.

He crouched as his gaze shifted uphill. "I spend all day trapping wildlife and putting up with bluffing fishermen, so don't begin to think you can walk or talk your way out of this." He pulled off his belt as his demeanor turned animal-like.

The inevitability of the violation weighed on her. Suddenly, the uniform she'd admired so much seemed an ineffectual barrier to her current threat. Pulling fresh air into her lungs, she made a quick break for the woodland edge, opening her gait by the fifth step to gain speed.

He tripped her with his boot and she flipped, tumbling out of control until she struck the base of a small tree. Ruthless, he twisted her right foot to flip her and it made a loud pop.

White stars filled her vision. She struck back with her free foot, but he caught it, pressing it under his knee. Before she could sit up, she felt the belt strap tighten around both ankles. That's when the dragging began.

Pushing up with her palms, she tried to clear the leaf litter and come up with a plan. Her upper body force proved no match for his, but she could still scratch and bite with a vengeance. When he lashed her to the base of a small bay tree, white pain shot up her leg.

He lifted her shoulders and threw her back against the trunk. She clawed at his face before he captured her wrists and tied them solid. Good, his cheek now bled from the scratch.

A short-lived victory, soon his shirt doubled over a branch and knotted to hold her captive. When he tried to force a kiss, she dodged enough to catch his upper lip between her teeth and bit down for all she was worth. He wrenched away with a roar and backhanded her across the face. The impact drove her head against the tree, where everything went black.

~

Court made the edge of the woods and realized he'd failed to bring a weapon with him. Pumping with solid adrenalin, maybe he wouldn't need one. Rawlings might be cunning, but with the lock gate open, he wouldn't be expecting anyone on this side for a full cycle.

He ran faster and heard a man's growl echo up the trail. Good girl. Fallon must be putting up a fight. Past a stand of pines, he saw the wetland clearing and heard a soft moan to the left.

A jerking action put him on full alert and then he saw her, strapped to the tree. His blood seethed and he lunged at Kit Rawlings with every ounce he had. As he knocked him off-balance, his right fist made solid contact on the man's jaw, earning him distance away from Fallon.

Seeing she'd been knocked unconscious, his rage unleashed. He kicked the attacker's feet out from under him and pummeled him in his fury.

Rawlings struck back and managed to twist out of his grasp, jumping to his feet like a cornered animal. Crouched, he launched a lightning-fast kick.

Before Court could dodge, it struck right under his chin. Something snapped and when he tried to lift his right arm to punch back, it hung limp as though it had detached. The advantage shifted to Rawlings.

~

Fallon knew this small bay tree. She'd meant to prune it earlier as the trunk that now held her was rotten. Having trouble seeing out of her left eye, she sensed that help had somehow arrived, distracting Rawlings for the moment. She shimmied the shirt loop out over the slender tree and collapsed her knees, using her weight to break the brittle trunk. The shirt now in hand, she untied the wrist shackle and, in seconds, dropped the ankle strap. Straightening in newfound freedom, she assessed the two men tumbling toward the wetland. *Lord help*. Court had come to her rescue.

She took a step toward them and almost fell face-first. Her right ankle wouldn't function. With pain arriving in white-hot arcs, she dragged the leg-stump, searching for her vest as she went. Court stood hunched and could only grapple from his left side. Disadvantaged, she'd have to re-enter the fray and push the balance back in his favor. Her pruning shears flashed to mind and she slid down the embankment under the boardwalk. There they lay, right where she had abandoned them. Charlie had sharpened the blades on his whet stone just this morning, so they were plenty sharp. That pleased her more than it should have.

Emerging with some leverage, she caught Court's attention behind Rawlings and nodded to his left side. His head twitched ever so slightly and she moved into position. Court lowered his left shoulder and bowled into his assailant, knocking him to the ground. She took a wild lunge, partially opening the blade to expose the cutting edges. The tool made landfall just over the attacker's right hip, pinning him to the ground.

Court grabbed her arm, heaved her over his left shoulder, and ran out of the woods.

Her head throbbed with every step, but she braced up to get one last look. Rawlings writhed on the ground, attempting to remove the buried blades. Relieved, she relaxed her arms. The next lunging jolt brought wraparound head pain. "Not gonna make it," she muttered, as her field of vision went white. Court's one-armed grip tightened around her torso as black snuffed out the rallying sensation of escape.

~

From the causeway clearing, Court spotted Charlie up on the tower platform with a rifle in his hands. Fallon moaned and he slowed, glancing behind him. The sentinel waited a few seconds and moved inside where a bell rang that led to the closing of the north lock. The lock shift created his escape route off the causeway. His jaw ached, but that didn't compare to the hurt registering deeper inside. Fallon's blood-smeared face haunted his thoughts. Dread spread to his lungs. He had to fight for his next breath. At least he had her now, ending the nightmare. Rawlings could rot like wormwood back there for all he cared.

Halfway across the pedestrian passageway, Liam and Sheri came running to meet him. Sheri fell in step behind, securing Fallon's head.

Liam gave him the once-over. "Charlie's already called the ambulance and the police. Is Fallon going to be okay?"

"I got there in time," he replied, clenching his teeth. When they didn't seem to line up right, he flexed his jaw and pain rippled up to his left ear.

Sheri sobbed. "Bless you, Court, for coming up today."

"I came to iron out whatever's been at odds between us and found something even more rotten." He stepped across the concrete flank and landed on real dirt. Searching for a shady spot in the grass, he shifted Fallon off his shoulder and laid her down with Liam's help.

"She overheard you tell your neighbor that you didn't need a girlfriend," Sheri said with a sheepish look. She fanned her hands over Fallon's face as her first tear slipped out. "I tried to tell her you didn't mean *her*. Still, she took it pretty hard."

Charlie emerged from the tower, his expression chiseled.

Court fought through the guilt of the latest revelation to come to terms with the situation.

"I think he broke her ankle intentionally, so she couldn't run for help." Unable to look her senior officer in the eyes, he took a moment to beat himself up further for being so oblivious. A boat motor roared to life under the lock to cut off his negativity.

Liam ran to the railing. "The fisheries boat—it's headed up the canal."

Court regarded Charlie and something went unspoken between them. "Go call Andy at Port Mayaca lock. Tell him Bait Crate will take that favor now." Court hung his head as the old man disappeared into the tower. An ambulance screamed up the access road and he found himself at the hub of an accident scene all over again, a familiar routine. He knelt by her side until the EMTs approached.

Time ticked by, but he barely comprehended it. Standing, he watched them load Fallon in the ambulance. He soon felt Sheri's hand on his shoulder as they closed the doors.

The driver faced him and made a clinical sweep of his frame, head to toe. When he reached out to shake hands, Court couldn't respond with his right hand. "You're in with her, pronto," the EMT said, pulling the doors back open. "Take either side by your girlfriend there."

"I want the right side, so I can hold onto her," he replied, sensing the inevitable. The attendant nodded and reached for his good elbow to give him a hand up.

The last thing he saw before the doors pinched closed was Sheri's tear-streaked face pressed into prayerful hands. "Tell Andy not to let him get away," he shouted through the crack, knowing there was nothing more he could do. A blood pressure cuff tightened around his left bicep and he leaned back against the cot.

Fallon came to with a moan and turned toward him as the vehicle started to roll.

"Hey, thanks for having my back out there in the

swamp," he teased, wanting like crazy to touch her. The rip on the corner of her eye looked frightful with encrusted blood. Regardless, his woman had prevailed under threat of evil. Something beeped and the cuff went limp. As soon as the EMT had it off, his hand trespassed over to her gurney. When his thumb found the hollow of her neck, her hand joined it with a faint squeeze.

"Good teamwork, lock runner," she replied, her narrowed gaze searching his face.

Before the attendant could restrain him, he rolled toward her and planted a rescuer's kiss on her swollen lips.

"Watch her head trauma," the medic warned.

"Keep us together in the ER," Court replied, his eyes loving on every inch of her face.

A trained hand palpitated his right shoulder and lifted his arm. "We'll keep you together in surgery, too. Broken right clavicle. You no longer have the use of your right arm."

Court winked at her and rolled back onto his cot, exhaling the last tension out of his trouble-fraught system. "So *now* you tell me. No great wonder I had to be rescued by a girl."

The EMT snickered as he prepared a sling for the limb while Court laid there like a ragdoll. The ambulance pitched as it made its way onto pavement and accelerated toward the hospital. He winced and clamped his left hand over Fallon's.

Chapter 22

Fallon stepped into the church's nave, blinking to adjust to the dim lighting. A piano plinked out a classical score as black-clad attendants mingled near the doorway. Her parents entered behind her and she positioned her crutches to walk the aisle.

A man laughed as quick-handed antics transpired between groomsmen. There stood Court, being strangled by his own arm sling. He shrugged out of it and punched the air near his brother. Carter dodged his retaliatory swipe and the laugh repeated. He'd found a way to make merry in the aftermath. His sister was getting married today, a day full of joy.

"Cut the shenanigans," Warren barked with mock authority.

She giggled and tried to advance toward the sanctuary, but Court locked on them in two steps and had her by the elbow. "I'm sorry, Miss McKenzie, but Callie doesn't want any slings or crutches marring her wedding photos, so we'll have to divest you of those back here."

She frowned until it pulled at her stitches too hard. "But how will I make it to my seat?" She gave him a moment to assess her outfit, as she'd worn his birthday gift to her for sentimental reasons. It looked like she had passed inspection when a coy smile curled his lips. Carter tugged at her crutches and she relented, grabbing the left elbow extended by the dapper elder brother. A sight for aching eyes, the black tux carved an impression on her memory and she tried hard not to blink it away.

"We can take it slow, my damsel-no-longer-in-distress. It's a wedding, after all." Court winked over his shoulder as Carter took her mother's arm and her father dropped behind them.

She had to put more weight on his arm than the average guest required, but the sensation of walking the aisle with Court exceeded any other half-baked apprehensions she could concoct. Despite her injuries, she felt radiant. Naturally, he escorted her all the way to the front. She poked his ribs at the second row and he halted.

"Slide down the pew so you can see me better up front," he teased, giving her a second to navigate the turn. When she tried to brush him away, he caught her hand and raised it to his lips. A lens shutter responded and a wily photographer winked over his camera. Another picture clicked as Carter deposited her mother. Court tapped his vest over his heart as he dropped back from the end of the row. Warren stopped him briefly and the men exchanged whispers. She tried not to conjure up a conspiracy, but the day seemed poised on trigger-touched emotion and half-hidden imagery. She sat down and drew the ankle cast forward. How ladylike would it be to prop her leg up on the pew cushion?

Lattice work draped with peach tulle formed a focal point up on the platform. White baskets with delicate-looking alpine flowers anchored a central set of steps where the bride and groom would ascend to exchange vows and light their unity candle to dispel the darkness of a solitary existence. Her mother smiled when Court reappeared, stepping down the pew's length. She leaned forward and looked at him, questioning his return.

"I'm only doing half my job here," he admitted, shoving some folded papers at Warren. He passed them down and she received a lovely wedding program with the order of service detailed inside. The cover featured the bride in a lush garden, a Bible in her hand. "Like Callie's going to fire me or something," he quipped, sticking a finger under his bow tie.

She giggled and swept him away with the program, then used it to hide her blush. Lord have mercy, she'd regressed to a giddy school girl all because of a handsome man in a tux.

The church filled up over the next fifteen minutes. The music switched to something more lyrical where the notes cascaded over the precipice of anticipation. A set of grandparents were brought in on the far side and Brian appeared up front with the minister. Court came down with his mother on his arm and she saw the heightened emotion on his face, which triggered her tear well to start producing. She sighed and reached for the tissue her mother offered.

Carter brought Tessa down next and she sat right in front of Fallon, her hair tucked up with ringlets framing her face. He paused a moment to bestow adoration on his wife and straightened to return to the parade. Four women in peach-colored sheath dresses measured their steps down the aisle next, as the groomsmen made their way down the far side.

A longing tugged at her heart to have Court closer and Fallon squirmed in her seat, unable to do anything about it. When he took his position up front, she had a direct view which relieved the pain a little. Her ankle winced, a reminder that she had no business standing.

The bridal march started and a curly-topped Nikki bounced down the aisle to her own rhythm, tossing rose petals in bronze and peach to litter the bride's path. In an unmeasured march, Cayden followed, his pillow only slightly tipped. He stopped in front of Brian and nodded.

Fallon studied Court's love for his family. Before she noticed the procession, Callie had traveled down half the aisle, blazing the trail of matrimony in a pouf of pure white chiffon. The moment proved that the pendulum did have an upswing, and it was incredibly mesmerizing.

~

From the noise ricocheting off the fellowship center's walls, Court thought the entire congregation had attended Callie's wedding. Fighting the picture-perfect image of his plan, he resisted putting on the tux jacket. The peach punch sloshed in the goblet he carried as he turned his attention back to Fallon. She sat sideways at the table reserved for his family, her foot now propped up conspicuously, though she tried to hide the cast with her long satin skirt.

Warren drew something of a map on his dinner napkin. Bent, his father scrutinized every detail. His mother shared his niece and nephew with Janine, who couldn't seem to get enough of their cute antics as they darted to and from the table.

Carter had moved off to a side table and seemed deep in conversation with his wife. Tessa laughed at something he said and tilted her head like a teenager in search of attention. Carter leaned closer and took her hand, entwining his fingers. In response, she placed her other hand over his. Next, he lunged over the table for a full-fledged kiss that made Court ashamed he'd been watching. No doubt about it, God had begun taping something back together over there. Good thing Liv and Janine could keep the kids at bay.

"Ah, my refreshment returns," Fallon said, reaching for her punch refill.

He slid it into her grasp and dried his fingers on a discarded napkin. A sprig of baby's breath stolen from the centerpiece now found its home in her hair.

She caught him noticing and glanced up over the rim of the glass. She swallowed and the little pearl dangling from her choker flaunted its position at the base of her neck.

If his plan worked out, that little gem might be out of a job real soon.

"Fallon, did you hear?" Liv asked across the table. "Court plans to let Callie and Brian live at his place."

Fallon's astonished gaze traveled from her back to him.

Court shuffled his feet. "You said it yourself. Remember? There's a time to retain and a time to relinquish. I'm letting go of the coast."

Her face flushed. "But where will you live?"

"The bride's ready to toss her bouquet," the

photographer said, motioning to the platform beyond the cake table.

Court gave him a thumbs-up and turned to collect his hindered guest. He had formulated a course of action to set the stage. All Fallon had to do was show up.

She raised both hands like double stop signs in opposition to participating in the tradition. "No, Court. I'm sitting this one out. My foot is killing me."

"Ladies, if you'll follow us, please," he requested, scooping Fallon up in one fluid motion He carried her to the bouquet landing arena. Liv brought Nikki who skipped to bounce her curls. Janine shot a chair under his load once he got her into proper position.

"Court, I'm sorry this isn't very lady-like of me, but this right foot has got to go up."

"Not a problem." He strode to retrieve a second chair, worried that a maiden seated with her foot propped up might not be in the best position to snag a flower-filled fly ball. Several peach-clad bridesmaids meandered into the all-female flock. Callie soon stood before them, flinging kisses to family and friends. He caught the look of unmitigated joy on his sister's face and hungered for something similar with all his heart.

One glimpse at Fallon in her lowly position made him snap into action. Desperate times called for desperate measures. The photographer motioned the mob to move forward and bunch together. He shoved Fallon's chair closer and she waved him off, resigned to be on the fringe. Not to be undone by a last-second logistical complication, Court stepped into the feminine gaggle just off Fallon's knees. The photographer leaned into Callie to make a comment and his sister gave him a little wave. A couple of groomsmen fired verbal jousts in his direction, but he held his ground. They had a catch to make.

Callie turned her back to the crowd and peeked over her shoulder one last time as though taking aim. The bouquet launched strongly to one side. All he had to do was box out two skinny bridesmaids and tap the bundle straight into Fallon's lap. He readily got the assist and she ended up with the bouquet in her hands. *One down and two to go.*

He kissed her forehead as she admired the flowers and inhaled their scent. Stepping out with the groomsmen, he followed Brian to the stage's edge, stopping to shove his little brother out of the pack. "I think you're claimed—or should I say reclaimed?" he teased, punching him in the arm with his left hand.

Carter mocked a payback strike and Court dodged him like a boxer. Dropping his shenanigans, Carter patted his chest and nodded.

Court received it as a blessing, knowing he had his family's backing on this.

Brian called a quick warning and shot a black garter off his index finger. It took a short arch over the masses but, being the tallest of the lot, Court didn't let the unfortunates get their hopes up. He crimped the satin band in his fist and smiled at the photographer. *Two down and a big one to go.*

On cue, Jim lifted a red velvet chair onto the stage as Warren escorted Fallon up front. Court met the bride and groom at the base of the stairs and exchanged hugs and high-fives. He turned and there stood Fallon, astonished and blushing. His tip now paying dividends, the photographer rushed to the platform edge and insisted on the traditional picture of the bouquet recipient with the garter bearer. He shrugged his shoulders and laughed, taking her elbow. Brian helped and they got Fallon to the throne-chair center stage. By the time he knelt in front of her, the lump in his throat exceeded the diamond's bulge lurking in his pocket.

~

By far the most comfortable chair she'd sat in today, Fallon settled into place and let the demanding photographer have his snap-happy gratification. She posed the bouquet against the embroidery of her blouse to maximize the style and gave Court a few seconds to get organized with the garter. She tucked her broken ankle with its hideous bootie under the chair and made her left foot available for his gallant deed.

Court hesitated and she heard her father cheer him on, followed by several more. The photographer snapped a shot of her alone and backed away at an angle to capture the garter exchange.

Court looked up at her with a fixed gaze that short-circuited time. Expressing his gentle preference, he guided her fat ankle forward and stretched the black satin band around the toes of her bootie, blowing a kiss to lock it in place. The photographer shifted on the periphery as the lens clicked. He rose to stand, only to reach into his pocket and slide closer on bent knee.

Her satin skirt quivered across her knees, as tradition's antics now seemed to travel into dreamland, a place where she had forbidden her thoughts to venture. Nikki appeared with a cute curtsey, borrowed the bouquet, and left her empty-handed in the moment.

"Fallon McKenzie, today God's pendulum of time swings in a brand new direction. The relinquishment is done and now it's time to retain. No more catch-and-release for me. I found a keeper and it's you. Will you stay and love me until the end of time as my devoted wife?" His fingers unclasped to reveal a simple platinum-set diamond solitaire, its mount slung in a curve like a spoon lure.

Hesitating to draw a full breath, the pause must have stretched longer than she'd intended. Little Cayden made an appearance off his uncle's shoulder, coonskin cap in place and mouth open. Nikki stepped close enough one of her garland ribbons tickled her shoulder. Court held his place, eyes expectant on hers. She lifted her hand, took the animal skin hat, and transferred it from nephew to uncle. A flicker of recognition warmed Court's gaze.

"I do and I will," she replied, sliding her right hand down the coon tail and across his jaw. He took her left hand and fitted the ring in place. She pulled him against her chest in a bonding hug as the lens shutter went off like a heartbeat. Cheers wrapped the rafters as Court slid his cheek against hers and sealed their agreement with a lingering kiss.

The coonskin cap disappeared with a tug from a toddler's knuckles and she laughed, cupping Court's face in her hands. "Ready to nest, lock runner?" she asked, a good-natured tease needling through her joy.

"Just let me get this wing healed up, so I can carry you over the threshold in both arms," he replied. The photographer approached and made him shift behind her, his good arm crooked around her neck. Nikki returned the flowers in time to add a suitable backdrop for her diamond. When Court whispered a promise into her ear, she laughed like a woman with no regrets. The camera clicked and captured a photograph she would treasure. She had lifted her lock runner, and this time, the heart he saved had been her own.

256

Epilogue

Autumn glinted off the waters of Lake Okeechobee, lending a golden tint to Fallon's veil as she peered over the edge of the floating dock at her reflection. A railing of tulle twisted around fishing nets pressed against her fitted skirt and held her onto the matrimonial platform. She needed a groom for the rest. Her gaze searched the stand of water oaks Court had disappeared into only minutes ago.

Family members and friends sat landward of the dock, stirring with anticipation. The cowboy preacher cleared his throat and nodded as Sheri appeared up the gangplank, clutching slender stems of yellow roses. Andy, her escort, took a seat on the second row with a shrug of his shoulders. Water lapped under the dock edge, calming her in the elongated wait.

The bow of a rowboat appeared from the vicinity of the boat ramp, and soon it became apparent where Court had been hiding. Carter alternated strokes with his older brother in the stern and the boat brought its suited occupants toward the dock. Her heart made buoyant at the sight of her intended, Fallon stepped beyond the makeshift altar and turned her back to their guests. Flowers adorned the bow, overlaying the dark wood with lace-like delicacy. Carter tossed her the bow line and she reverted to her daily task with an unsuppressed grin.

The best man stepped onto the dock and motioned toward the boat, arresting her humor. Feeling a tug at her elbow, she found the cowboy preacher nudging her toward the vessel while Sheri stole her bridal bouquet. Her dress train found the crook of her elbow as Court stood in the boat, offering her a hand. With his eyes searching her face, Fallon accepted his hand and made the transfer into the small craft. It wobbled under the weight shift and he secured her into his arms. An insistent shoulder tap broke his transfixing gaze as her bouquet found her hands again. Court turned her around to face the altar.

"Dearly beloved, we are gathered here today to unite this man and this woman in holy matrimony," the preacher said. "This is a blessed day for Fallon and Court, two strangers brought together along this waterway, now here to become united as one under divine authority with you as witnesses upon the ample waters of Lake Okeechobee."

"Welcome to heaven," Court whispered through her veil, leaning against her with the slightest brush. She lifted her gaze to the shimmering waters and dropped one hand from the bouquet, searching for his behind her back. He connected and she drew a breath, certain they were heaven bound and journeying there together, latched by undying love.

The End

Nature writer Cindy M. Amos spent over a decade living in the subtropical wilds of South Florida before coming to the Midwest to share her stories. Working as a field biologist with native flora and fauna, she hung up her binoculars to become a stay-at-home mom to her two adorable sons. Living along the Intracoastal Waterway in Hobe Sound, Florida, Ms. Amos launched many daytrip adventures to teach the boys lessons about nature. Though the beach was their favorite destination, she often trekked up the St. Lucie Canal to the fascinating lift locks operated by the U.S. Army Corps of Engineers. With alarms sounding for the boaters and water soon swirling into the locks, a thrilling atmosphere always greeted them. A closed lock meant an open nature trail, which the boys learned all too quickly. Lake Okeechobee, placid and ever-tempting as an aqueous escape route, suitably portrays the natural tranquility of palm tree-studded Florida. Ms. Amos now makes her home in Wichita, Kansas and ranches in the expansive Flint Hills, where the season-led wildflowers bloom in endless arrays.

Find more on her website
http://cindymamos.wixsite.com/natureink.
Like us on Facebook at
https://www.facebook.com/Cindy.M.Amos.23

<u>OTHER BOOKS BY CINDY M. AMOS</u>

LANDSCAPES OF MERCY SERIES

Book One   *Redeeming River Rancher*

Book Two   *Saving Bicycle Man*

Book Three   *Justifying Sound Strider*

Book Four   *Sanctifying Ace Aerialist*

NATIONAL PARK ROMANCE SERIES

Everglades Entanglement

50 STATES COLLECTION

Secondhand Flower Stand